HAUNTING SEASON

HAUNTED EVERLY AFTER MYSTERIES
BOOK EIGHT

REGINA WELLING
ERIN LYNN

Willow Hill
BOOKS

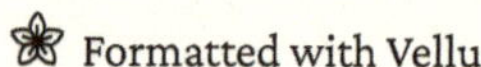 Formatted with Vellum

CONTENTS

HAUNTING SEASON

CHAPTER ONE

A furious buzz of gossip replaced the silence that had fallen over Cappy's Tavern while Ernie Polk marched Patrea Evergreen out the door in handcuffs. My heart raced as I looked at the plate she'd barely touched and realized she must have known something was up because she'd been acting oddly during our Friday night get-together.

"What the hell just happened?" Jacy pitched her voice loud enough to be heard over the crowd.

"Someone call Chris. I have to get to the station." I rose to leave, but when I grabbed my purse, pain flared in my wrist, making me remember I hadn't driven to the bar because of my injury.

"Go!" Neena waved a dismissive hand. "I'll take care of the bill and meet you there."

"Um, you both rode with me, remember? Nobody's leaving until I do." Jacy scanned the bar for signs of our server and motioned for Miranda to bring the check. "We'll settle up first, and then we'll go. A few extra minutes won't make Patrea any less arrested."

Patrea had been arrested for a murder I knew beyond

a shadow of a doubt she didn't commit. How could I possibly be so sure?

Fun fact about me—I see ghosts. Specifically, I see the spirits of people who have been murdered, and the only way I can get them to leave me alone is by finding them justice. Had justice truly been served in this case, I'd be standing in a ghost-free zone instead of shivering from the proximity chill and wondering how to get one of my best friends out of trouble.

How to do that without revealing my deepest secret was the question.

While we waited for the bill, I called Patrea's husband, who could not have picked a worse time to deliver potted pines to a big customer in New Jersey.

"I heard," Chris answered without a hello. "I'm packing up and heading back now. Tell her I love her, and I'll be there in eight hours or less." He hung up.

I tucked my phone into my purse and pulled out my debit card to pay for dinner. "Chris knows, and she wouldn't have had time to call him yet, so the gossip mill's running at warp speed." Which shouldn't have come as a surprise given the sea of speculative faces turned our way.

Conversation hushed along our path but picked right up behind us as we passed through on our way toward the door. This was not one of those wind-in-the-hair moments where a group walks confidently into battle, but

I did stare down a couple of the more gleeful-looking customers on my way by.

"She didn't do it." Jacy took defiance a step further. "So you can stop talking crap about Patrea. Right now," she raised her voice, her tone going harsh with annoyance and sounding overly loud in the sudden lull when the song on the jukebox ended. "Get a life, people."

Several people had the grace to look chagrined, others shrugged off the admonishment and continued to stare, but one man did neither. Face red, he rose and shouted, "I say give the girl a medal because she did the world a favor! Thou shalt not suffer a witch to live."

"Sit down, you old coot, and shut up." The man's table companion, a woman I didn't recognize from the back, grabbed his arm and gave it a yank when he didn't immediately sit. "Nobody asked for your opinion." I didn't recognize her voice, either. The outburst served to change the tide of popular opinion a bit. More people called for him to hush up.

Some guy near the bar yelled, "You've got one hell of a nerve judging anyone else." Such undisguised anger colored the statement. I craned my head around to see who spoke but couldn't tell.

A roar of agreement rose from the crowd. The instigator of chaos responded by going even redder in the face. "Don't you even talk to me," he said, his voice shaking. "I know all your dirty little secrets." He leveled a shanking hand and pointed toward the bar and other spots around the room. "Cheat, adulterer, liar, killer, thief."

I wasn't the only one glancing around the room to figure out who the man was talking about. Small towns run on gossip, and Mooselick River was no exception to the rule, especially when Friday-night regulars made up the majority of the crowd.

Darcy and Nelson Campbell sat at their usual table, and for once, they didn't seem to be in some stage of a fight. Probably because they'd been joined by the unlikely couple of Thea Lombardi, Jacy's replacement when she'd left the diner, and Jason Todd, the chef and chief bottle-washer at my friend David's new business, The Marlow Inn.

Why hadn't any of us noticed that before? It would have made for interesting dinner conversation trying to figure out what those two might have in common. Jason was a nice man with some miles on him, while Thea tended toward surly most of the time. I lost track of the excitement for a moment, trying to figure out if they were there on a date or not. They'd take the prize for the weirdest couple of the night if they were.

When one of the bouncers glanced at the bartender and tilted his head toward the furious man's table, Milo answered with a head shake, rounded the bar, and went to the table instead. With a great deal more restraint than I would have used, he spoke to the upset man, got him to settle back into his seat, then looked deliberately at those still buzzing until things went quiet again.

"That's enough," was all he said. Then he stalked over, dropped coins in the jukebox, and punched the buttons decisively until a popular song began to play. "Eat, enjoy the music, and keep your opinions of others to yourself." With that, he returned to take a slew of new drink orders while Adam, the cook who had come out to check on things, went back to the kitchen.

"Who was that guy?" I asked when we'd cleared the door. I didn't recognize him, but Jacy would know. Years of slinging hash at the local diner put her in contact with just about everyone in town.

"Jober?" Jacy gave the name a Downeast spin, so it sounded like Joe-bah. "Jober Peavey. People call him Oddjob, though."

I frowned. "Why?"

"Because he does odd jobs. Duh." Neena earned herself a half-hearted glare. "I know he helped Mrs. Willowby with her flower beds sometimes, but Hudson wouldn't hire him."

"How did I not know about this guy when I was crawling through cobwebs to thaw pipes last winter? Seems like someone could have given me his number."

But Jacy was shaking her head. "Leo wouldn't have let you hire him. They have beef. Or they did a couple of years ago. Got into it in the diner one day over something to do with Mabel. I didn't hear the whole thing because it happened before Leo came out of his shell, so it was the quietest fight ever if you know what I mean."

I did because when I took the property-management job for the soft-spoken and mild-mannered Leo Hansen, he'd been too shy to yell for help if his butt caught fire. But one day, he had what you might call an epiphany. After crushing on Mabel for years, he decided it was time to let her know—got himself a makeover, went down to the diner, and sacrificed his dignity on the altar of love by singing her a song.

Jacy shrugged. "Other than that, all I know is Jober moved here from somewhere down-state right after you took off for the big city. He's a picky eater and a crappy tipper." She gave me the salient points as she saw them, based on prior experience as a server at the Blue Moon Diner.

In the car, we put the whole Oddjob incident behind us and refocused on the major drama of the night when Neena echoed Jacy's earlier sentiment. "Patrea didn't do it."

Since the not-nearly-departed-enough dead psychic Patrea had supposedly murdered hadn't moved on and now hovered over the seat next to Neena where I was the only one who could see her, I tended to agree. "Patrea isn't a killer, but Ernie mentioned finding prints on the neck-lace used to strangle Davina, so I assume they were hers. I wonder how that happened since she never mentioned an interest in books of the....esoteric variety, and I can't think of any other reason to go to the bookstore. Wouldn't you think Davina would go to Patrea's office if she needed legal help?"

Davina quirked a brow at my choice of words, which I'd hoped would be a prompt for her to say something useful for a change.

"We had private business. That's all I can say without breaking psychic/client confidentiality."

Not useful. Shocking.

Jacy hit the gas hard, spun up a spray of gravel, and rocketed out of the parking lot in her pink bullet of a mini-van. I grabbed for something to hold onto, and so did Neena. Davina merely chuckled, but I happened to get a glance back at her as the van jigged sideways, and the ghost spent a moment half inside the car and half out of it.

Not so funny now, eh?

Her hand gripping the door handle, Neena made a dry comment. "I didn't think these things had the giddy-up to spin the tires like that."

Glancing in the rear-view, Jacy grinned. "I had my father-in-law give her a few tweaks to get a little more power out of her. He changed out the standard for a cat-back exhaust, installed K&N filters. Air induction..." She trailed off when she noticed Neena's eyes had glazed over.

"You realize you're speaking some sort of car geekinese, right?" Neena brought the conversation back to the more important topic. "Maybe Patrea visited Davina for professional reasons. We don't know her all that well. Maybe there's someone missing from her past, or else she could have been doing some legal work."

"Her brother," I said as the memory flooded back and the pieces fell into place. "His name is Justin, and he ran away from home as a teen." Using Neena as an excuse, I spun in my seat so I could see Davina's face as well. "I bet Patrea asked Davina for help finding him."

Davina nodded.

"Doesn't explain her fingerprints being on the murder weapon," Jacy mused. "If that's even what happened."

Neena flipped a curl of chestnut behind her shoulder, her dark eyes troubled. "You don't think she could have done it, do you? I know everyone has their breaking point, but I can't see Patrea getting riled up enough to commit cold-blooded murder. She's too..." Neena hesitated, then chose, "controlled."

Since I knew the whole story but didn't want to share anything told to me in confidence, I said, "She wouldn't kill over anything to do with her brother, but if she did, it would have happened a long time ago, and to the person she feels responsible for the situation." Namely, my ex-husband, Paul. "I can't see her going after Davina for not being able to find him after all these years."

Davina shrugged and cut her gaze away from mine.

The next opportunity that presented itself, I had some questions about her history with Patrea.

"I spoke to Chris. He's already on the road but won't make it back until mid-morning," I said two hours later when Ernie finally buzzed us into the inner workings of the station. Patrea, looking miserable in orange, huddled on a bench in the single jail cell.

"Did you bring my purse?" was not the first thing I expected to come out of her mouth.

And, of course, I hadn't thought to grab it when we left the bar. None of us had.

"I'll call the tavern and check if they found it," Jacy went out to make the call in private while I pulled out my checkbook.

"How much to cover your bail?" To my embarrassment, I had plenty.

Patrea lifted a brow, rose, stepped close to the bars, and would have grasped my hand through them if Ernie hadn't growled. What color her face had regained washed right back out, leaving her pale.

"That's not how it works, but I appreciate the offer." She went back to her seat and sat with her shoulders rounded. "There has to be a bail hearing first, which won't happen over the weekend."

Don't blame me. I hadn't exactly had a lot of experience with jail or bail etiquette.

"Then what can I do?"

"We," Neena corrected me and rose to let Jacy back in, ignoring Ernie's beetled brow. "What do you need?"

Patrea allowed a ghost of her normal grin. "What I need is less important than what Ernie needs, and that's a reality check." She raised her voice slightly, "I didn't kill Davina Benet."

"Of course, you didn't." Jacy shot Ernie a glare. Neena and I followed suit. "Anyone who thinks you did is wicked stupid."

Ernie stood stalwart under the insult unique to Mainers, directed his gaze to each of us in turn, then confirmed my earlier theory. "Only someone wicked stupid would ignore the evidence. Her fingerprints were on the murder weapon."

"How?" I turned back to Patrea, hoping for an explanation, but she shook her head. Probably best if she exercised her right to remain silent until her attorney showed up. "Never mind. I don't need to know because I'm not wicked stupid."

All the good feelings and respect I'd had for Ernie Polk evaporated as, I suspected, did his for me. The man didn't appreciate being called stupid, but I didn't care. If the dunce cap fit...he was welcome to wear it.

"Lay off the poor man." Surprisingly, Patrea defended Ernie. "He's just doing his job."

"Fine." But Jacy crossed her arms and glared in his direction anyway. "He's not doing it very well," she muttered.

"Put your checkbook away." Patrea leaned forward on the uncomfortable bench and rested her elbows on her knees. "Bail won't be set, and the bonds office won't open until Monday at least, so unless you can pull the actual murderer out of your butt in two days, I won't be going anywhere until then."

"There has to be something we can do." Being powerless to help didn't sit well with me. "Anything."

Patrea's head came up and swiveled toward Ernie. "Well, there's one thing, but it depends on how much of a…"

"Jackass?" Jacy supplied while Patrea searched for a more diplomatic term.

"Stickler Ernie wants to be," Patrea flashed Jacy a quick smirk. "In my purse, there's a roller bottle of essential oil. Leandra gave it to me to help with my monthly cramping issues."

Confronted with three identical expressions of surprise, Patrea flushed. "What can I say? I've been assimilated into Momma Wade's flock, but the stuff actually works, and I don't mind smelling like spice and flowers one week a month."

Ernie's face reddened but being duty-bound, he couldn't leave the room until we did. According to the clock on the wall above his head, we'd already missed the chance to get back to Cappy's before closing time.

"If we leave now, we might make it before Milo locks

up for the night," Jacy said. "Are you sure that's all you need?"

Patrea nodded, and I didn't think I'd ever seen her look so alone. "I'll be okay."

If I had anything to say about it, she would. I'd found killers before. I could do it again. Probably not before the bail hearing, but what else could I do but try?

CHAPTER TWO

Not even a half hour past closing time, the bar portion of Cappy's was already dark, the parking lot empty of all but a broken down truck that had occupied one corner for so long tall grass poked through the pavement around it.

"We're too late," Neena said, yawning. "Have to wait until tomorrow, I guess."

Jacy shook her head, spun the wheel, and aimed the pink bullet of death toward the back of the tavern. "Milo won't have gone home yet. They lost their regular dishwasher last week, so he and Miranda have been taking turns putting the place to bed. See, there's his truck." She pulled up behind an old Toyota pickup with some of the letters painted out so across the tailgate, it read, YO.

"Okay, I'll run in and grab her bag. Shouldn't take long." I'd already slung the door open and grabbed onto the frame with my good hand. At least this was something I could do for Patrea. Probably the only thing tonight.

The back door opened into the end of the kitchen with deep sinks and the hulking presence of two industrial dishwashers--neither of them running--and a pair of dirty pans waited on the drainboard.

It didn't occur to me that something was off until I called out for Milo, and he didn't answer.

When I didn't see him in the kitchen, I walked through the double doors, flipped on the lights, and strode into the bar proper. A quick check turned up Patrea's missing bag on a shelf behind the counter. I scribbled a hasty note to say where the bag had gone and that it was in safe hands and propped it up on the register. It wasn't like Milo to leave the place unattended.

"Everything okay?" I raised my voice slightly and tried again. The utter quiet suddenly felt unnerving. "Milo!"

Dead silence followed as the echo of my call faded away.

"I swear, if you've gone and got dead on me, I'll kill you," I muttered without thinking of the statement's absurdity. But the dread settling in the pit of my stomach told a different tale. I'd been down this road enough times before to listen to my gut.

"What's taking so long?" Jacy popped around the corner, Neena right behind her. "Did you find it?"

I held up the purse. "Right here."

"Well, let's get going, then."

"Not so fast. I found the purse, but I can't find Milo."

Jacy's eyes widened. "He can't have gone far. Milo wouldn't leave the door unlocked and take off. He's not that type of person."

"I know." That was what had me worried.

"Milo!" Jacy yelled as if I hadn't tried that already. More than once. "Where are you?"

"If I had a flashlight," Neena said, her face going pale. "I could take a look around outside."

"There's one in the glove box of the car," I said. Like me, Jacy always kept a flashlight, a battery wrench, some fuses, and a tire patch kit in her car. Not that I actually thought either of us could patch a tire, mind you. But my father had drilled into us the need for keeping what he considered the basic necessities handy. There was also a first aid kit, a set of jumper cables, and a battery-powered air pump in my trunk. I'd be willing to bet Jacy had the same things stashed somewhere in hers.

"But don't go out by yourself. If something has happened to Milo, it's safer if we stick together."

"Okay." Neena let out the breath she'd been holding and nodded. "You're right. Safety in numbers and all that." Still, she walked around the back of the bar, selected a firmly-corked bottle of wine, and held it by the neck as a weapon. "Shall we?"

Calling out Milo's name periodically, we wove through the tables and checked the utility closet.

"He's not in there," Jacy stated the obvious, her eyes round with worry after returning from one of the restrooms.

"Not in here, either," Neena popped out of the other.

My gut jumped when we got near the kitchen again,

so I wasn't the least bit surprised to smell the coppery tang of spilled blood when I opened the pantry door. Why hadn't we looked here first? Instead, we'd wasted precious minutes searching the front of the bar while Milo's time might have been running out.

"Call Ernie. Tell him I think someone's dead." I ordered over my shoulder, then closed the door in Jacy's face. She didn't need to see whatever it was I was about to find, and neither did Neena. Neither did I come to that, but it was too late for me now.

Turning away from the door, I moved deeper into the storage area, passing a stack of five-gallon pails of pickles. A single bare bulb barely lit the back of the room and walking into the cool dimness felt like walking into a cave. A pair of legs stuck out past the far side of a shelf loaded with condiments in large cans with brightly colored labels.

"Oh, Milo. What's happened to you?"

When I rounded the corner to get a good look at his face, I realized it wasn't Milo at all and let out the breath I'd been holding.

No answer came, and it wouldn't have mattered where we began our search. With his eyes fixed and staring and a kitchen knife sticking out of his back, I could tell the man who'd yelled at us earlier, the one with the funny name, was already gone.

Or was he?

I mean, he was definitely dead, but the dearly

departed don't always dearly depart. At least not in a timely fashion. The murdered ones preferred to stick around to become a thorn in my side, and Oddjob clearly hadn't accidentally stabbed himself in the back. Or I didn't think he had, anyway. It's not like I solve crimes for a living or anything. Plus, I was trying to look at him without really looking at him, if you know what I mean.

"What's going on in there?" Jacy pounded on the door I'd locked behind me. "Did you find him? Is Milo okay? Let me in!"

"I did not. I don't know where Milo is, but I hope he's okay. Give me a minute." Preparing myself mentally, I scanned the scene in more depth. Saw the trail of blood suggesting the victim hadn't died quickly or easily or where I'd found him. He'd crawled some way and tried to leave a clue before succumbing to his injury.

Sirens wailed in the distance as I pulled out my phone and snapped a few photos of the crime scene. I didn't notice I was shedding them until a tear splashed on my phone. Careful not to contaminate the evidence any more than I had already, I framed a shot of the two X marks on the side of a whiskey crate that this poor man had managed to draw using his own blood. When I was done, I opened the door, went out, and closed it behind me.

"It's definitely not Milo, but there's a dead guy in there, all right. Stabbed with a kitchen knife. It looks brutal, and you don't need to see it. We'll let Ernie handle things from here." Unless a ghost shows up, and then I'll be forced to investigate—I left that part unsaid, but given the look Jacy shot me, she didn't need to hear those words to know they were true.

Paler than before, Neena stared at me. "I still love you, Ev, but seriously, you're like a tragedy magnet."

No kidding.

Jacy brushed past me and yanked on the handle. "Who is it?"

"It's Jober Peavey from when we were here earlier." I raised my voice over the din of the sirens getting close enough to be loud and followed her back. So did Neena. "At least, I'm pretty sure it is. I didn't look that close, and I only saw the guy once from across a crowded room."

Sober-faced, Jacy stared down at the dead man. "It's Oddjob, all right," she confirmed. "Where's Milo, though?"

"I don't know. Come on," I said, grabbing her arm and pulling her away. "Ernie gets cranky when someone disturbs a crime scene."

"Ernie gets cranky if the Gas-N-Go runs out of break-fast pizza by two in the afternoon. It doesn't take much to get Ernie cranky." But Jacy let me guide her out of the storage room and close the door behind us.

"Everly Dupree," Ernie called as he entered the kitchen through the back door. "I know you're in here."

I stepped into sight from around the corner.

"Just because there's a dead body doesn't mean it was

me who found it," I said, ignoring the truth of the matter out of pure pettiness.

"When is it ever not you?"

"Jacy called it in. How do you know it wasn't her?"

"Was it?" He tilted his head and gave me a steely stare.

"No." I fought off the urge to sulk. This really wasn't the time. "It was me. He's in there."

"Milo Lynch?" Ernie frowned as he made to step past me.

"No," I turned and led him back to the pantry door. "It's not Milo." He followed me inside. "It's Oddjob Peavey, and before you ask, I have not touched anything. None of us did."

Being careful not to disturb the position of the man's body, Ernie did the obligatory check for a pulse.

"Any witnesses? Where's Milo?"

Poking fun at Ernie was a favorite hobby, but he did the job. I considered him a good cop and a good man even if we annoyed each other on the daily. "I don't know. The place was deserted when we arrived."

"Milo's truck is parked outside." Ernie straightened from his crouched position next to the body. I didn't like the speculative look on his face.

"You don't think he did this, do you?" Jacy hadn't followed us into the storage room, but that didn't stop her from listening at the door with Neena. "I've known Milo for most of our lives, and I just can't see it." She came around the corner, stepped into the pantry, and waved a hand when Ernie began to speak. "I know what you're going to say: everyone has the capacity for murder given the right circumstances. I think that's a load of—"

"Jacy," Neena cut her off. "Let the man do his work."

"I'm not stopping him, am I?" Jacy rounded on Neena, the stress of the situation bringing out a tendency to snipe at each other in the sisterly fashion they'd developed since opening their shop together. "And speaking of Milo, shouldn't we be worried about him? I mean, his truck is here, but he's not. We searched the whole place so we'd know if he was. There's obviously been a struggle, and if he didn't kill this guy, then where is he?"

"Even if he did," Neena ignored Jacy's killing glance, "Someone ought to be looking for him before he gets away."

Before Ernie could answer, the demanding tone of a ringing phone split the air, and we all looked at each other to see whose it was.

It wasn't mine. Both Jacy and Neena shook their heads when I gave them a pointed look, and since Ernie didn't move, I guessed it wasn't his. Turning, Jacy locked in on the source of the sound and disappeared from the doorway. Seconds later, the ringing cut off, and I heard her say *hello*, then *hang on*.

Then, she was back. "It's Milo's wife. This is his phone, and she says he should have been home by now." She handed the phone to Ernie.

"Ernie Polk," he began, then cut off, his lips twisting. "Mrs. Lynch, please calm down."

Why is it that certain people never realize *calm down* is a phrase that usually has the opposite effect? Frowning, Ernie pulled the phone away from his ear, punched the button to turn on the speaker, and gave us all a chance to hear. It probably didn't help that the ambulance Ernie had called was just pulling into the parking lot, and the sound of the siren came through the bar loud and clear.

"Mrs. Lynch," Ernie said again with a sense of futility.

"He's dead, isn't he? You tell me right now." Milo's wife began to cry with great gusto while Ernie reached up and tugged on his ear.

"We don't know anything yet, Mrs. Lynch. If you could, please just listen for a moment. We have no reason to believe Milo has come to any harm, but there's been an incident at Cappy's. His truck is here, but we are...uh... unable to ascertain his current whereabouts at this time."

The crying slowed. "Is that fancy speak for you don't know where he is?"

"That is the situation," Ernie confirmed. "Can you tell me when you last spoke to your husband, Mrs. Lynch?"

There was a short pause. "He called me right before closing to say he wouldn't be late, and now, you're telling me his truck, and his phone are there, but he's not." There was no sign of tears in her voice now.

"Well, he'd better have a good excuse when he gets home." Milo's wife hung up on Ernie, who stared at the phone for a moment, then handed it back to Jacy as the paramedics entered through the kitchen door.

"In there," Neena motioned toward the storage room and then stood back to give them room to bring their equipment inside.

"I'll have to ask you ladies to clear out of this area," Ernie said, "but don't leave just yet. I'd like to get your statements while everything that happened is still fresh in your minds."

One of the paramedics called the time of death, and Neena's hands shook, so I didn't argue. "We'll be out there." I waved a hand toward the front of the tavern. "Whenever you're ready."

CHAPTER THREE

"I'd better call Brian and tell him why I'm so late," Jacy pulled her phone out and walked a short distance away for the sake of privacy. Since Neena just stood staring, I flipped the chairs down from the nearest tabletop, righted them, and got Neena settled in one. Under the circumstances, I didn't think the management would mind if we dirtied a glass or two, so I went behind the bar for three sodas. I'd have liked a good slug of brandy in mine but figured Ernie wouldn't appreciate it if I fuddled up my brain.

"Aren't you going to call Drew?" Neena gestured with her glass. "It must be nice to have someone waiting at home who cares if you're going to be late."

It was the first time she'd expressed any interest in having a man around since the death of her husband a year ago.

"I'm sure he's already gone to bed, but I'll text him in case he wakes up and wonders where I am." I picked up my phone and typed in a message, then frowned in surprise when Drew answered right back, asking if I was okay and if he should come to the tavern.

"That's sweet." From across the table, Neena read the message upside down. "You've got a good one there."

I nodded as I sent a message back to say thanks, but he didn't need to come. "I do."

Not more than fifteen minutes later, Ernie pulled out the fourth chair at the table, spun it to straddle the seat, and took notes while we gave him the rundown on our evening exploits.

"Aren't you worried about Milo?" I wanted to know. "He could be lying dead somewhere, too."

Leaning back in his chair, Ernie gave me a measured look. "I've got an APB out on him and deputies combing the area as we speak. I do know how to do my job, you know."

Heat flamed over my face. "I know, and when did I ever say different?"

CHAPTER FOUR

"**G**et some sleep." Jacy put a hand on my arm to keep me getting out until after Neena had walked across the street and staggered up her front steps. "Oddjob?" She glanced into the back seat. "Is he…you know…with us?"

"Not yet. But Davina was with us leaving the bar, and now, she's sitting on my front porch." I'd been too distracted to notice at what point she'd gone off to wherever ghosts go when they're not bugging me, but she was back. I was too tired to deal with her. Not that she cared.

Jacy sighed, then perked up slightly. "Maybe she can help you figure out who killed Mr. Peavey. Or at least help us find Milo. Or can she still do that sort of thing now that she's dead?"

Well-known as a psychic gifted with finding missing persons, Davina Benet had left Mooselick River to ply her trade all over the world, eventually ending up with her own TV show. When she'd retired earlier in the year, she moved back to town and opened up the shop where I'd found her strangled to death with one of the beaded necklaces she kept in stock.

Before Ernie settled on Patrea as his prime suspect, he'd brought my mother in for questioning because she'd been a driving force behind a protest against Davina. In spectacularly bad timing, she and her group had marched in front of the bookstore less than an hour before the murder.

Maybe that was why, if her psychic ability survived beyond the grave, Davina hadn't used it to be helpful so far. I wasn't expecting anything different from her now.

The rising sun glinted off the single tear that rolled down Jacy's cheek. Poor Mr. Peavey and poor Milo. Barely married a year, and I had a bad feeling about him.

"I'll ask," I promised. "For now, go home and hug that baby for me."

Inside, Davina followed me to my sunny, yellow kitchen, where I found Drew already up and studying a set of drawings for a possible expansion of his fitness center. A flurry of paperwork covered the table. My dog, Molly, sprawled under it, her head resting on Drew's foot.

"Hey, babe. You okay?" He rose, skirted around the dancing dog, and pulled me close. For a moment, I relaxed into his warmth, took a couple of deep breaths, and let the clean scent of his skin lull my nerves. The sense of security felt amazing until the import of the evening's events rushed back. I quivered in his arms and couldn't hold back a sob.

"Long night, huh?"

"Horrible. First, Patrea gets arrested, and then I find another body. Worst night of my life."

Drew pushed me to arm's length, his face a sympathetic mask. "You should have let me come."

"There was nothing you could do." It was only then that I noticed the fatigue around his eyes. "You waited up for me? All night?"

"I catnapped in the recliner." Was that a touch of disappointment in his voice? "I thought you might need me."

"I did. Do. Knowing you would be here when I got home was everything." Laying one hand on his scratchy cheek, I curled the other around his neck and pulled his head down for a kiss. I would have done more, but we weren't alone.

"Meet me in the bedroom later," I whispered against his lips.

"What about here and now?" He kissed me again.

You'd think Davina would take a hint and leave.

You'd be wrong.

"I need a minute to settle." I dropped my forehead low and snuggled up under his chin to keep him from kissing me again.

"Later, then," he all but growled.

After several more precious seconds, I pulled free and busied myself filling the teakettle. While I selected one of Leandra's special, soothing herbal tea blends, I gave him the expanded version of the evening's events. He'd had the highlights in a series of quick texts but needed to hear the whole story.

Putting aside the subject of the new death for the moment, Drew focused on the more personal connection to the previous night's events.

"Patrea's not a killer."

"I know, but her print was on the murder weapon. Ernie did what he had to do." I didn't have to like it, but that much was true.

Trying to be helpful, Davina stayed silent until I finally settled in the chair opposite Drew and said, "Davina's going to tell us everything she knows about Patrea so I can figure out the best way to help her. Help both of them, really."

"Davina's here?" Drew looked right through her as he scanned the room for some sign of a ghostly presence, and it dawned on him why I'd put off his very welcome advances.

"She is. She won't be able to tell me everything I need to know, and you should be prepared for what could happen. Ghosts tend to freak out when they try to talk about their deaths. If she does, you might feel the vibrations." I gave Davina a pointed look but held up a finger to keep her silent until I'd given Drew the salient points about Patrea's brother and his disappearance.

"Now." I turned to her. "Tell me everything you know about Patrea Evergreen."

"I've known Patrea for a couple of years," Davina

began. I repeated the statement for Drew's benefit, earning an impatient look from the ghost. "One of my missing persons needed help with a legal matter, and she came highly recommended. Nothing that had to do with my death, so I won't go into detail, but that's how I met Patrea." Again, I repeated what she said.

"Enough!" Davina waggled a finger at me and then closed her eyes to concentrate. Drew let out a choked sound and pushed his chair back away from the table, his eyes trained on the dead psychic.

"You're...that's...you're a ghost, but I can see you."

"Good, since that was kind of the point. Davina Benet, nice to meet you."

When Drew failed to respond, she snapped her fingers at him.

"Hello. Can you hear me?"

His eyes went round, and his breathing sped up. "Yeah." He slapped a hand over his heart. "I'm just...give me a second to get used to this, okay?"

"No time for that. Showing myself to you like this takes some work, so I'll need to make this fast. You'll just have to keep up."

Drew nodded and, under the table, reached for my hand. "Go ahead." He still looked dazed. I knew exactly how he felt.

Still, his acceptance must have curried favor because Davina grinned. "Hang onto this one. He's scared witless, but he's sticking. Man's got some stones."

Drew choked and turned red while I barked out a laugh. "Oh, I know," I agreed with Davina's assessment. "He's a keeper."

If possible, Drew blushed harder.

"Get on with it," he muttered.

Davina turned pensive. "Not all of the missing are meant to be found. Some are escaping an abusive home life or may be suffering from a guilty conscience that preys on the mind until there seems to be no other choice but to leave everything behind. Some leave for reasons that seemed valid at the time and then, after a while, have simply been gone so long that they don't know any other way to be. I never considered it my place to judge."

"Patrea's brother fell into one of those categories?" Patrea's family didn't seem the abusive type, nor had she mentioned anything along those lines. Unjustly accused, Justin hadn't cheated in school, so the guilty conscience seemed a stretch. "He was scared of his family's reaction if he came home?"

"Not exactly."

I wanted to roll my eyes so hard I could see my brain from the inside, but I stomped on the impulse before I could act on it. Pissing off ghosts is a bad idea. Sufficiently motivated, they can wreak the kind of havoc that ends with your furniture stacked like Stonehenge. After the night I'd had, I didn't need havoc. My nerves couldn't take it.

"What category did he fall into, then?" I pressed on

the spot Leandra would call my third eye to release some of the tension gathering there. "I'm too tired to play verbal tennis. Just tell me if you know where Justin is? And did you tell Patrea?"

"Yes, and no." Davina tilted her head. "More no than yes. I mean, I knew he was safe, but that's really all I got from him. So I told her she'd have to wait for him to decide if he wanted to make contact."

"How did she take that news?" I blew on my tea to cool it and took a sip.

"About like you'd expect. She was happy to know her brother was still among the living but upset that he couldn't find it in his heart to reach out."

After clearing his throat first, Drew jumped in. "Everly mentioned Patrea's fingerprints on the murder weapon. Can you tell us how that might have come about?" His eyes were still a little rounder than normal, and his fingers worried at the lower hem of his tee shirt, but Drew did his best to take the situation in stride.

Taking a moment to think first, Davina finally said, "She came in maybe half an hour before the picket line got underway. We talked about her brother. I told her as much as I could and what I thought she should, or rather, shouldn't do about it. She wanted more details, but I held firm. She got emotional, and we both had a little cry."

Picturing Patrea in tears brought the sting of them to my eyes. She was the strongest woman I knew. The type for whom tears never came easy, so she must have been in a great deal of pain to show such vulnerability to Davina. I wasn't sure if it made me sad for her or angry with her that she hadn't said a word to me at a time when I could have given her some support. Mostly, it left me feeling powerless to help in a way that I didn't like.

"Anyway," Davina continued, "when I reached across the counter to offer her a consoling pat on the hand, I knocked several pieces of merchandise on the floor. Patrea helped me pick up the mess. That's probably how her fingerprint came to be on those beads."

Sounded innocent enough, and I assumed Patrea had already explained the situation to Ernie. Still, this wasn't information I could corroborate to clear Patrea's name without inviting questions. If I'd had any doubt about Patrea's motives or innocence, Davina's ability to discuss that portion of her final day among the living dispelled them.

"Good to know, but there's no way to prove that's what happened." I tapped my fingertips on the table and framed my next question carefully. If I touched on anything pertinent to Davina's death, she'd go poof on me. "Did anyone else come into the shop while Patrea was there?"

"Did you see her leave?" Drew asked at the same time.

Thinking back didn't so much as give Davina a shiver. I let out the breath I didn't know I was holding. "Yes, I walked her out the back and locked the door behind her.

She didn't want to go out the front with puffy eyes, and by that time, the protesters had arrived."

"But she could have circled around, waited until the coast was clear, and come in again." The statement delivered in Drew's thoughtful tones earned him a hot glare from me.

"You do realize that if Patrea had actually committed murder when Ernie took her into custody, Davina would have gone into the light. Not ten minutes ago, you were convinced of her innocence. Do you really think she's capable of murder?"

Davina cut in. "Everyone's capable of murder given the right circumstances."

"Yes," I got huffy. "Ernie says that all the time, but you haven't described anything like the right circumstances, and I know Patrea. She would never resort to using her bare hands. She's too invested in upholding the law. Now, if you could literally kill with words, and she had a really good reason, that would be a different story. And even then, if she was ever pushed to the point of actual murder, she's the type to look a person in the eye, not sneak up behind them."

Drew reached over to pat my knee under the table, but I yanked it away. Traitor.

"I didn't mean to cast aspersions. I know Patrea didn't kill anyone, but we must consider everyone a suspect until we learn something that rules them out completely. Davina's continued presence in the face of Patrea's arrest certainly appears to rule her out, but would that be the case if she wasn't acting alone?"

I stared at him as if he'd grown a demon head in addition to his own.

"Fine. Let's examine the *im*possibility, then." I mocked his tone and turned to Davina. "You said Patrea arrived ahead of the protesters, and you spent some time together discussing her brother's disappearance. Is that right?"

"Yes."

"Was she alone?"

"Yes."

"Did she act shifty or suspicious in any way?"

"No."

"Did she seem angry?"

"Not at all."

"Not even when you talked about her brother's disappearance? Did she push back when you couldn't tell her where he was?" Before the words were out of my mouth, she was shaking her head.

Davina pursed her lips. "No, nothing like that. She was more upset with him than with me." She turned to Drew, "your theory is crap, by the way. For Patrea to be in cahoots with someone, she'd have had to plan ahead or call someone when I didn't tell her what she wanted to hear. I don't know about you, but I have...had friends I could call to go out for drinks on the spur of the moment, but none who'd jump right in and kill someone. Maybe you have different friends."

When Drew's knee brushed mine this time, I didn't pull away. Davina had schooled him pretty hard.

He swallowed twice. "After Patrea left, what did you do?"

"Watched the protest with Leandra." Davina's eyes sparkled. "Such fun. I thought the whole thing was a hoot, and it was going quite well until Gloria and Martha got into a shouting match over the Halloween event. The church folk remained quite respectful, but Gloria was mad for not being asked to host a booth at the Halloween thing. She was hoping to generate awareness for her association. Once she admitted her problem was with the event planning and not with me, Martha offered her a booth in a prime spot. Gloria flipped like a trout trying to get back in the water."

Davina grinned. "You should have heard her berating the church group. She called them all a bunch of narrow-minded bigots, then dragged her cronies away, and the whole protest fell apart."

Nodding with his head cocked to one side, Drew said, "Were you in fear for your life at any time during the protest?"

The laugh bursting from Davina's lips came with a wash of chilled air. "Not for mine, but I half expected Martha to grab a picket sign and start whacking people."

Not entirely out of the realm of possibility.

"No, I wasn't scared. I had no reason to be. My work tended to generate strong opinions in people. They either found it intriguing or thought I was a fraud. There was very little in-between. If I couldn't get used to that, I shouldn't have been using my gift, anyway."

Hers might be a gift. I still considered mine a curse.

"When things quieted down," Davina continued. "I figured that was it for business for the rest of the day. I finished tagging merchandise, then settled in the reading nook with a mystery that had arrived in the morning shipment. Good book, too. I'm annoyed I didn't get to finish it. It was about these two witches who move to a small town, open up a shop, and solve murders."

Sounded like a fun read, but that wasn't the point. Knowing it might make her jitter and fade, I went ahead and asked, "What happened next?"

Davina blinked, then closed her eyes to picture the scene. "Let's see. The front door opened and closed—there's a bell so I can hear when customers came in—I called out to say if whoever it was needed help finding anything, just ask."

When she paused, Drew prodded, "Did they respond?"

Frowning, Davina said, "No, actually, and that's odd since most people do. I heard footsteps, smelled funeral flowers, and then I was dead."

Paranormal energy flickered across my skin as Davina's whole body shivered twice, then solidified again. I had to hand it to her, for a ghost, she had serious staying power.

"Funeral flowers?" It seemed like an odd description to me. "Like lilies?"

She shrugged. "If lilies smell sort of spicy."

"They don't." Drew wrinkled his nose. "They smell sickly sweet. Cloying." He shuddered.

I guessed I wouldn't have lilies in my wedding bouquet, then.

"I've always envied Leandra her green thumb," Davina said. "I can tell a daisy from a rose, but that's about the extent of my horticultural aspirations. Whatever it was, it made me think of a funeral. Later, I figured it was all part of my transition to this side of the veil."

"Okay." Drew rubbed his forehead and repeated, "you heard someone come in, but they didn't speak, and you didn't see your attacker, but you smelled spicy funeral flowers. Probably carnations. Aren't they used in casket blankets a lot?"

Having attended more than my fair share of funerals of late, I considered. "Yeah, that sounds about right." But debating what flowers Davina might have smelled wasn't getting us any closer to clearing Patrea's name.

"Have you made any new enemies recently? Received threatening mail? Found anyone who didn't want to be found?"

Tension set into the muscles of my neck and shoulders while a little voice in the back of my head began placing bets on how much longer the ghost could hold out. Plus, it seemed as if we kept going over the same old ground. But the stakes were higher now. It wasn't about getting Davina out of my hair or about her claim she could stop my personal hauntings. Patrea's freedom was on the line, and I needed more than bits and pieces of information if I was going to finally find a motive for Davina's murder.

"Define recently." Davina seemed as solid as ever. "Enemies is a strong word, but I'll admit I ruffled a few feathers in my time. You don't solve kidnapping cases without ticking off a perp or two. I've refused to pass on information that would lead abusers to their victims. My job wasn't all about getting my face on TV."

I started to let the TV comment go by because she sounded defensive—no sense in getting her all riled up—then rethought the decision.

"What can you tell me about the process for getting on the show?"

Quirking a brow at me, Davina thought for a moment, then frowned and said, "I see where you're going with this, but more than half a million missing persons cases get filed yearly in addition to cold cases already on the books."

Drew seemed surprised. "That many?"

Davina nodded. "Statistically, eighty percent of the children are found within a day, and seventy-five percent of the adults as well. Still leaves a lot unaccounted for, but plenty of people don't believe in psychic phenomena. We got scads of letters asking for my help, and that's on top of people who just showed up to wait in line for each taping."

I couldn't imagine what I'd do if one of my parents went missing, to say nothing about any child I might have. Panic topped the list, and panic combined with time would most certainly lead to desperation. Desperate people are more likely to do desperate things.

"You're thinking a potential client from the show followed me here and did the dirty deed?" Davina tilted her head to think.

"Not a potential client." I tapped fingernails on the table while I worked it through. "Or maybe, but the logic doesn't hold. I can see someone following you here to try and get you to come out of retirement, but killing you just means they'd never get your help."

My tea had gone stone cold, but I sipped the last dregs from the cup while Drew nodded thoughtfully. "I don't know. Failure to secure your help might have been a trigger if the murderer was already close to the edge."

Davina didn't appear convinced. "A fine theory if anyone had come asking, but no one did."

"When was your last kidnapping case?"

"Too long ago to matter, and we didn't accept those cases on the show. Kidnappings were strictly a police matter. I helped by invitation only or didn't get involved at all. I wasn't one of those movie psychics haunting the station to get the authorities to listen to me. Except for that first time, anyway."

Davina cocked an eyebrow and watched Drew lean back in his chair to grab a notebook and pen from the junk drawer without getting up. He flipped open the cover, found a blank page, and made a notation. From across the table, with the book upside down, I couldn't read what he wrote, but Davina seemed to know.

"All of my kidnapping cases made the news." She turned to me. "I assume you've looked them up on the web, so all these questions are moot."

"I have looked you up online," I admitted. "Nothing jumped out at me."

"What about family?" Drew wanted to know. "The... um...method of the crime strikes me as personal. Any friction with your loved ones?"

Davina shook her head, but I saw some deeper emotion flicker in her eyes. "There's my brother and sister. Tim's the youngest. He was what you'd call a menopause baby. An afterthought. Then there's me in the middle and Mina's older by three years. But we all got along well enough that I decided to move back home to spend more time with them. Guess that didn't work out too well, did it?"

"Guess not." She'd begun to turn pale around the edges, so I rushed Davina through the last of my questions. "Any other family?"

"Just the in-laws. Mina's been divorced...it must be going on twenty years now. Tim has a lovely wife and a couple of little ones."

"No cousins? Maybe the odd aunt or uncle waiting to pop out of the woodwork?"

She shook her head. "If I had any aunts or uncles, I can assure you they would not be more odd than people find me, but I don't. No cousins that I know of, either."

"Okay. Can you help us find Milo?"

Her pale edges went transparent. "Maybe, later. I think we're going to have to be done. I'm—"

"Gone." Drew let out a gusty breath. "That was intense."

When he stood, I let him gather me in and rested my head on his shoulder. "I'd understand if this kind of thing is too much for you."

His arms banded tightly for a moment, then he held me away so he could look me in the eyes. "That was one the coolest thing that ever happened to me. I just talked to a real, live ghost."

I couldn't help but grin. "Technically, that would be a real, dead ghost."

He kissed me.

"I have to work today, and you should get some sleep."

As much as I agreed, Patrea's purse still sat on the table. "I just need to drop some things off for Patrea at the police station. Once that's done, I intend to come home and take a nap."

He kissed me again and left for work.

I really did have the best intentions, but as usual, life had other plans.

CHAPTER FIVE

*I*f, according to my mother, everything happens for a reason, then fate must have poked my ribs with its bony finger because I was standing at the front desk of the police station at about an hour past the buttcrack of dawn with Patrea's purse clutched between my fingers when Milo Lynch stumbled through the door.

He looked like he'd been hit by a car, or maybe just a hammer. Dried blood darkened his collar from white to a rusty brown. His hands looked like crimson gloves. As he walked past me, I noticed a small rivulet of fresh red dribbling from a cut over his eyebrow and a larger streak tracking down his neck. His eyes were wild and dazed, and he wobbled a little.

"I must have done it," Milo shoved past me and slapped a hand on the counter in front of Carole Ann Wilmette as much to keep from falling as for emphasis. "I've come to turn myself in."

When he wobbled again, I reached out and grabbed his arm. "Milo, I think you should sit down. You look just awful." With a glance at Carole Ann that I hoped she would interpret as an order to get Ernie in here as quickly as possible, I tried to guide Milo to the nearest seat.

He wasn't having any of it and firmly but gently dragged his arm out of my grasp.

"I'll sit down when I'm locked up where I belong." Turning to Carole Ann again, he wrung them, then held out his hands. "I thought it was just a bad dream, but I remember seeing a man's legs, and there was blood. Look at my hands. Don't you know what that means?"

Quietly for once, and wasn't that a wonder, Carole Ann keyed up the two-way radio system and contacted her boss.

"Ernie's on his way, but you're hurt, Milo. Please, come and sit down." I stepped in front of him to get his full attention. "You're bleeding."

"I am?" He checked his hands, lifted one to the side of his head to touch a spot behind his ear. "I must have cut myself." When he looked back up at me, his eyes had gone blurry. "Is it bad? Is my truck okay?"

"Carole Ann," I kept my tone pleasant. "It looks like Milo needs medical attention." She nodded and made another call. This time, he let me get an arm around his waist as I tried to guide him toward the nearest chair.

"Did I have an accident? I can't remember. Do you know what happened to me?" Milo blinked twice. "My head hurts." His eyes rolled back, and he slumped forward. I managed to break his fall but only just. The man was heavier than he looked and dead weight besides.

"Ambulance is on the way." Carole Ann came around the corner of the tall desk and looked down at the prone man. "So's Ernie. You think we should put cuffs on him?"

My left eyebrow shot up. "I don't think we're authorized for that."

"But he confessed to murder. It's up to us to do something, isn't it? Like, make a civic duty arrest or whatever it is."

"A citizen's arrest, you mean?" You'd think she'd be familiar with the term, given she worked at the police station.

"Whatever you call it." She nudged him with her toe. "If he killed someone, we can't let him leave."

"Does he look like he's trying to leave? He's obviously hurt and needs our help." I stripped off my jacket, draped it over Milo for warmth, and made a mental note to suggest Drew find someone to give a First Aid course at the gym. I'd be the first one to sign up, and I'd bug Ernie until he made Carole Ann attend.

Looking past Carole Ann to the front window, I saw the patrol car pull into the drive. "Ernie's here. Let's let him take care of making the arrest if he feels it necessary, shall we? I think making sure Milo's okay should be the first priority."

"What's going on?" As usual, when he saw me there, Ernie scowled. I was getting used to ignoring his reflexive response but knew my days of flirting my way out of a traffic ticket were long gone. His gaze flicked to Milo, then back to me even as he hunkered down to check for a pulse.

"He's not dead," I said, and it came out defensively. "We've already called an ambulance."

"He said he killed that guy," Carole Ann put in her two cents. "Right in front of us, he confessed to murder."

Ernie rubbed his forehead, then pinched the bridge of his nose. Bloodshot eyes with bags under them that could hold a week's worth of groceries told me he probably hadn't gone home to sleep. I probably didn't look much better for the same reason.

"Is that right?" While Ernie looked at the other woman, the question was for me.

"Not exactly."

"Not exactly, my ass." A little spit came out when Carole Ann got fired up. "He said, and I quote, 'I did it. I killed a man in cold blood'."

At that point, I'd been awake for more than twenty-four hours—long enough that my insides felt like they were no longer connected to my outsides, and my patience had worn so thin you could read the newspaper through it.

"Have your ears lost their connection to your brain? That's not what he said at all."

More spit flew. "Don't think you can come in here and try to make me look like a fool," Carole Ann raised her voice to be heard above the din of the siren as the ambulance wheeled up in front of the police station.

"I don't have to try. That's something you manage all on your own, thank you very much." I turned back to Ernie and caught the faintest hint of a smirk before he smoothed it quickly away. "What he actually said was, "I thought it was just a bad dream, but I remember seeing a man's legs, and there was blood. Look at my hands. Don't you know what that means?"

"See? He confessed."

Ernie flinched, and my head throbbed as the dispatcher's shrill tone cut through the final bit of my patience to tap dance on my last nerve.

"How did you even get this job?" I snapped as the paramedics came through the door. Carole Ann tried to kill me with a look, but I was too tired to care. "You really suck at it."

"At least death and destruction don't follow me wherever I go."

I'm sure my next insult would have been a flawless piece of prose, but I didn't get the chance to utter it because Ernie busted in on the argument.

"Why are you here, Everly?"

"I wanted to let Patrea know I found her purse. She was asking for this, and I thought you could give it to her." I reached into my pocket, pulled out the essential oil roller bottle, and handed it to Ernie.

Brows raised, he handed it back. "That's contraband. Not gonna happen."

I should have shut up. I was too tired to care about

shoulds and *should nots*. With an exaggerated motion, I unscrewed the cap, waved the bottle a little too close to Ernie's face, and with the scent of carnations lending spicy sweetness to the air, applied the oil to my own skin and then to the wrist of the hand he'd put on my arm.

"See? It's harmless, and you smell really good right now."

If the paramedics hadn't chosen that moment to ask me to move while they got Milo on the gurney, I suspect I might have ended up in the cell next to Patrea for assaulting an officer of the law with a floral substance. As it was, Ernie snatched the roller bottle out of my hand, then the cap, mated the two forcefully, and with his gaze pinned on mine, handed the oil off to Carole Ann.

"Give that to Patrea." He ignored her miffed expression, waited until she'd buzzed herself through to the cell area, then turned to me. "If you're done being a giant pain in my ass, I'll follow these guys to the hospital. Do me a favor and call Milo's wife. Tell her whatever you think is best about the situation."

Nodding, I clamped down on the impulse to advocate for Milo again. It almost worked, too.

"You know what I don't remember seeing in that storage room last night? Anything the dead guy could have used to bash Milo in the head. Think about that before you pull a Carole Ann and assume he's guilty."

"Are you telling me how to do my job?"

One of the paramedics held out my jacket, and I took

it, hugging it to my chest. "I'm not. Or if I am, it wasn't my intention. I respect you, Ernie. Maybe not your choice of co-workers, but when it comes to the job, I do. I already told you that."

A day's growth of stubble rasped as Ernie scraped nails over his cheek, then he nodded. "Okay," he said, turning to follow as they wheeled Milo out the door. "Just make the call, and then, for the love of all that's holy, butt out. Of everything."

He swung out the door without waiting for me to confirm my agreement, which I had every intention of giving so long as the dead man's ghost stayed off my radar.

I mean, ten whole hours had passed without a sighting. Maybe this would be the time my luck turned.

CHAPTER SIX

"She's not dead." Robin Thackery spoke without preamble as she waved a box of tampons across the checkout scanner for the third time. I'd come to the grocery store for a few essentials, then planned to go home and sleep for at least a week.

I wanted to point out she'd never get them to scan with the barcode facing up, but "Who's not dead?" is what popped out of my mouth instead.

"That psychic chick."

The psychic chick whose body I'd found? I begged to differ. "She's dead. Trust me. I was there, and I know what I'm talking about." Live people don't invade my personal space or give off creepy chills when they get too close or make deals with me to get me to solve their murders.

"Except, she's not. I saw her in town yesterday and again this morning." Gum churned and snapped between Robin's teeth in a show that I found nearly mesmerizing.

Behind me, the next person in line at the grocery store checkout let out a sigh that said more than words ever could. I got it. I really did. Robin and reality lived on entirely different planes with no middle ground whatsoever. Every once in a while, though, she got something right. Not this, obviously, but just in general. Unless she'd developed the ability to see ghosts, too.

"I'm not the only one," Robin went on. She'd finally flipped the box of tampons over and got a nice beep for her efforts. Then another. Then a third. "Some say it's her ghost haunting the scene of her murder, but I saw her going in the back door to the town office this morning, and that was no ghost. Ghosts don't open doors. They walk right through them."

Beep. She scanned the same box again.

"Okay." It took iron control not to reach out and give her a shake for multiple reasons. "But it's not the second Saturday of the month."

"So?" Robin gave me a blank look.

"The town office isn't open...never mind, I guess I'll take your word for it." I ran my debit card through the scanner and held out my hand for the slip. I'd need it when I stopped at the service desk on my way out to get a refund for the three extra boxes of tampons I'd just paid for.

Those weren't the only things that added up funny during the shopping trip. My brain kept circling back to Robin's offhand comment about seeing Davina's ghost behind the town office, which was Martha Tipton's domain.

"I call shenanigans," I said out loud.

"Robin is the stuff from which shenanigans are made,"

came the dry comment from the store manager as he reached out for my debit card for the return.

He wasn't wrong, but she wasn't the only one in town cut from that particular bolt of cloth. If Robin had seen someone who looked like Davina going into the town office, that could only mean one thing: Martha Tipton was up to something.

Talk about shenanigans—Martha was their queen.

My plans for a nap changed abruptly. I gave Kirby a smile for his attempt at humor and stowed the groceries in the back of my car. At least I hadn't bought anything perishable—getting to the bottom of Robin's story might take a minute.

Who was I kidding? Anything to do with Martha Tipton would take a minute. Or ten. Unless I walked in on something shady. I did, after all, have a key to the town office's front door. She'd given it to me with great ceremony as she announced that since I was the most reliable person she knew, I was now her emergency contact, which included being in charge of her workspace if need be. Didn't matter that she had a family. I guess I was supposed to consider it an honor. I did not.

She hadn't heard me coming. A point in my favor.

"Hey, Martha." Her gaze cut toward the bathroom door before she plastered a welcoming smile on her face.

"What are you doing here? We're not setting up until tomorrow morning."

"I was out and about." I put on an air of innocence

when I could have asked her the same question. "How are the new glasses working out?" Gone were the cheaters dangling from a neck chain, replaced by a brand-new set of bifocals in plastic, cat-eye style frames.

"I hate them." The smile dropped to make way for a frown. "No-line, my left foot. I can see the line. Makes everything look like it's underwater." Martha tipped her head up and down as she peered at me. "The eye doctor says I'll get used to them. I sincerely doubt it. What can I do for you?"

She wanted me out of the way, that much was clear, but I ignored the subtle hint. "I actually came in to see what *I* could do for *you*. I realize Davina's death, and the whole brouhaha at Shady Acres has put something of a damper on the Halloween event, but it's tomorrow, and we hadn't talked in a day or two, so I figured I'd better check in."

When my former life imploded and I moved back home, Martha did me the huge favor of railroading me into buying the house known to children in town as Spooky Manor. Fully furnished and in really good condi-tion, the house turned out not to be haunted.

I am.

Not from anything Martha did, but I digress.

Actually, Martha did me a solid, and I'd been trying to pay her back by helping her plan a series of town func-tions to raise money and increase tourism. Bringing Mooselick River back to its heyday was her main goal. You had to give her credit for being altruistic. Didn't mean she wasn't a pain in my backside at times.

A mop or broom handle hit the floor behind the restroom door with a resounding crack. Martha did her best to pretend nothing had happened.

"Sorry, is this a bad time?" I asked.

"It is," Martha lit up like a stadium during homecoming. "I was just doing some cleaning. With Davina gone, it looks like we'll be going ahead with the same event plan as last year. We already have the tarps and signs in storage. Since your wrist put you out of commission, I've arranged for help setting up in the morning, so that's that, unless there was something else you needed."

Nice attempt to brush me aside. I wouldn't go easy.

"No, I'm good. Just checking for any last-minute changes. I'll just visit the restroom if you don't mind, and then I'll be on my way."

Martha nearly broke a land-speed record heading me off.

"I'm sorry. The floor is wet, and that tile can be slippery. I can't let you in there until it dries. Insurance purposes, you know." She sounded positively cheerful.

Well, two could play at that game. I crossed my legs and pasted a panicked look on my face. "I really have to go. I promise if I fall, I won't do anything litigious." Dodging past her, I headed down the hallway.

I got about two steps toward the door before Martha grabbed my arm and spun me around. "Insurance purposes." Iron-gray curls bobbed over wide eyes, her mouth set in a straight line. "I can't let you use the restroom. I'm sorry."

She really didn't want me to lock eyes with someone or something. Presumably, whoever Robin had seen entering the building.

"Okay," I put my hands up in surrender. "I guess I can make it home."

Relieved, Martha stood in the window and watched me walk back to my car. I cocked an eyebrow as I dutifully pulled away from the town office. I let her think she was rid of me, but as soon as I was out of sight, I hooked a right turn onto Water Street because it curved around behind the town office, parked, left the car running, and pulled a pair of compact binoculars from the glove box. Even with her new glasses, Martha would never see past the camouflage offered by the water district sign, but I still had a good view of the back door.

It didn't take long before Martha appeared on the back stoop. She looked left, then right, then left again, and once sure the coast was clear, motioned for whoever was behind her to come out of the shadows.

"Damn, Robin. I guess I really do owe you an apology," I muttered to myself when a woman who was very much alive and looked remarkably like Davina darted furtively from the doorway to a black, late-model sedan parked around the corner. From this angle, I couldn't get a look at the make, but it could have been any one of several since most newer cars look the same to me.

A chill stole over my skin a split second before the real…or would that be ethereal…Davina popped into the space to my left. It hadn't taken her long to recharge her energy.

"What are you doing?"

"Er…spying on Martha." I went with the truth.

Davina tilted her head, gave me a quizzical look. "Why?"

"A woman who looks a lot like you just sneaked out the back of the town office. My theory and I just came up with it, but I think it's good is that Martha found your double and hired her to haunt the town for the Halloween festivities."

In the grand scheme of things—grand schemes being the only kind Martha ever hatched—it wasn't the worst publicity stunt she could have done. With the right media push, it might even be genius.

Disrespectful as the day is long, but genius.

Davina clearly only agreed with the first half of that thought. Her face clouded over, and I heard thunder when she spoke.

"Delilah Cannon."

My scalp tingled as her pissed-off ghost energy rolled over me and stole my breath. "You know her?"

"Not half as well as she thinks she knows me." Her

disgust became a physical thing, rippling the grass around us.

"Settle down." Best if she didn't notice how her emotions could cause physical manifestations. "And tell me about her."

Settle down didn't work any better on Davina than calm down had worked on Carole Ann. She dialed her fury up to double, and the air took on the feel of a January cold snap. The hairs in my nose froze over.

Getting the story out might help Davina purge some of the stronger emotions. Or she'd get even more keyed up and turn me into an ice sculpture. It was a chance I had to take.

"Delilah Cannon claims to be my biggest fan." The response wasn't what I expected and did nothing to lessen the chill. "Biggest pain in my ass is what she is. Or was, I suppose. I'm still getting used to this being dead gig."

I murmured something vaguely soothing and let her talk it out, but I wondered why this was only coming up now instead of when we'd discussed possible suspects in her murder.

"Anyway, Delilah showed up for almost every taping of my show. It all seemed innocent at first. I thought she was looking for a lost loved one, but that was not the case. Then, one of the production staff mentioned she reminded him of me a little, and that's when things got strange."

"Strange, how?" I got a little tingle.

"The next taping, she showed up with a new hair-style." Davina pointed toward her head. "Same cut and as close to my color as she could get since mine is more of a rinse to cover having gone gray in my thirties. It's a family trait."

Didn't take a map and a flashlight to see where this was going.

"The birth of the doppelganger," I nodded.

"Pretty much," Davina nodded back. "Hair, then clothes, colored contacts, and I can't swear she had facial surgery, but she missed a few tapings, and when she came back, the resemblance seemed stronger."

"You didn't think this was information that might be useful before now? I'm trying to find your killer, and you keep holding out on me."

Fingers shaking from the cold and thanking my lucky stars that I'd had the foresight to leave the heater running, I tucked the binoculars back in their case and headed for the car. Davina followed, laughing but not in a *ha-ha funny* way.

"You're giving Delilah credit for having way more brains than she does. Besides, she idolized me. Why would she want to kill me?"

If I'd learned anything from my newfound experience with the recently departed, it was that the weirdest things could push a person over the edge of resorting to murder.

"Oh, let's see. Maybe you hurt her feelings, or she

thought you didn't take her seriously enough, or maybe she decided she was a better version of you? Seems to me if she wanted to take your place, getting you out of the way might be a good step in that direction."

"She hasn't got a lick of natural psychic ability and would be hard pressed to find her own backside if she had GPS, but I do see your point," Davina admitted.

It couldn't have been more than seventy degrees inside the car, but it felt like a sauna. I stashed the binoculars and held my hands in front of the blower, waiting for the heat to penetrate. The return of her sense of humor had put a damper on Davina's ice-making fury, so I had that going for me, at least.

Assessing, Davina fell silent for a long moment, only stirring to speak again when we'd pulled back into my driveway. "Or she showed up to pay her respects, ran into Martha, and got sucked in."

"Maybe," I acknowledged the possibility with a shrug. Short of an actual crime, there wasn't much I would put past Martha in her quest to better the town. "I'll pin Martha down and see if I can get to the bottom of things. In the meantime, can you check your closets to see if there are any more skeletons lurking in the dark depths?"

Davina waved the question away and smiled at me. Not the kind of smile that makes a person feel warm and fuzzy inside, her eyes glittered in a way that made my nerves twinge. "If Martha wants a haunting for Halloween, I see no reason she shouldn't have one."

Oh crap. What had I done?

CHAPTER SEVEN

I ran into Oddjob Peavey—not literally—at the Marlow when I stopped by on my way home. The encounter with Martha and subsequent chill from Davina had burned off some of the exhaustion but left me with a gnawing sensation in my belly. Jason Todd made the best Cuban sandwiches I'd ever tasted, and I was ready to beg for one if that's what it took.

Poor Oddjob sat on the front steps, his shoulders hunched, his head cradled in his hands. If I spoke to him, he'd probably latch onto me like a leech, but if I didn't, I'd feel like three kinds of a jerk for ignoring a soul in need.

"Jober?" I stood a few steps below him to bring us to eye level. "Jober Peavey?"

Do you want to know how you can tell the difference between a ghost and a regular person? For me, it's a dead giveaway when the ghost follows me home and sets up camp. Regular people hardly ever do that. In this case, neither did the ghost.

You'd think I'd jabbed him with a red hot poker the way he jumped and scrambled backwards up the steps to get away from me. The kicker came when he lifted his hands to make the sign of the cross at me with two shaking fingers.

"Get thee behind me, spawn of Satan."

Okay, I'd been called a lot of things in my day, but spawn of Satan was a first for me.

"Excuse me?" The shock sent me down a step.

"You're a ghost, and ghosts are of the devil. I don't hold no truck with the devil."

Good grief. What was I supposed to say to that? My mouth dropped open, but nothing came out, and by the time I finally did manage the brainpower to put two words together, he was gone.

"I'm the ghost," I muttered to no one and headed inside. "Doesn't that put studs in your snow tires?"

"Whoa, Dupree. You look like hammered crap." Always the flatterer, David Barrington owned the inn and had become a quasi-brother to me after my folks let him live in my old room during an emotionally trying time. Our fathers were good friends.

I rested my elbows on the counter he stood behind. "Thanks, Barrington. You really do know how to make a woman's heart go pitter-pat. It's a wonder you haven't been spoken for."

"You okay?" He dropped the banter and showed true concern. "I heard about," he waved a hand to indicate everything that had happened the night before.

My lips twisted. "You'd have to be living under a rock if you hadn't. Chris got the news about Patrea's arrest before the echo of the cuffs clicking on her wrists died out. The gossip mill fired up in record time. Hey, you haven't hired a guy named Jober Peavey to do any handyman stuff around here, have you?"

It had taken me a minute to come around to that maybe being the reason he'd been sitting on the steps. My brain still wasn't firing on all cylinders.

But David shook his head. "Wasn't he the one who was killed last night? The one they call Oddjob?"

I nodded.

"Nope. I tried to hire him when we were remodeling, but he said—he said this place was," David paused to remember and get the phrase just right. "As haunted as the day is long." He shrugged. "I've never actually laid eyes on the guy."

Well, there went that source of information. "I wish I hadn't, either. Neena called me a tragedy magnet."

At the mention of her name, David perked up. I'd thought something was budding between them, and he'd just confirmed my suspicion. Maybe it was time for some subtle matchmaking. They'd both lost someone they loved. They were both a little shy when it came to dating. A gentle push might not be the worst thing.

"She was pretty upset by the whole ordeal. Maybe you could pop by and offer her a sympathetic ear. Or take her to a movie to get her mind off so much tragedy. Buy her dinner. Maybe just not at Cappy's."

Not that the tavern would be an option for a day or

two anyway. Crime scene tape, blood pools, and forensics teams weren't great for business.

"What about you? Are you okay?"

I appreciated the concern. I wouldn't be nudging him in Neena's direction if David wasn't a stand-up guy. "I'm worried about Patrea and Milo more than anything. There's a scary amount of evidence against both of them. Patrea has a temper and was definitely in the wrong place at the wrong time. I don't know Milo all that well, but he's so affable, I can't picture him shoving a knife between someone's ribs."

Patrea's innocence wasn't even a question, but I couldn't say the same about Milo's other than I had a gut feeling about him. Or could I? Given the actual blood on Milo's hands, it was a sure bet Ernie had placed him under arrest, but Oddjob's ghost was still hanging around. That had to mean something, didn't it?

"Rumor has it he was covered in the dead guy's blood. I'd say that was pretty damning evidence, wouldn't you?" David echoed my thoughts.

"I suppose." One of these days, I'd probably have to confess my ghost-seeing abilities to David—especially now that my mother was in the loop. Today was not that day and wouldn't have been even if a cloud of heavy floral scent hadn't announced the presence of his resident housekeeper.

"Hey, Nanette. How's things?"

She shot me her lop-sided grin. "People are filthy

beasts, but if they weren't, I'd be out of a job, so things are good. I heard you had some excitement last night."

Below the edge of a bright blue bandanna tied over a mop of unruly curls, Nanette's brown eyes glittered with interest. She set her spray bottle on the counter, laid a damp rag next to it, and settled in to hear my story. Since fatigue had begun to drift back into my brain like fog settling over a valley, I went with the abbreviated version.

"He wasn't covered in the dead guy's blood," I ended my tale by refuting that particular piece of gossip, then damned Milo with an admission. "But he did have blood on his hands and at least one nasty gash on his head."

Nanette's eyes went wide while David's narrowed with speculation. "Both hands?"

I nodded, then closed my eyes to bring back the mental image. "What color was it?"

"The blood?" I frowned as David nodded. "Bright red. What other color would it be? Milo's not an alien." Beginning to feel punchy, I responded with sarcasm before thinking through the reason for the question.

David rolled his eyes. "Fresh, then," was all he said, but as a former EMT, he'd picked up on something I hadn't.

"Oh." The light dawned dimly. "Right. I get where you're going. If the murder happened right after closing time, and Milo turned up at the station this morning, the victim's blood would have had time to dry."

"As blood dries," David said, "it gets darker and darker

because the hemoglobin breaks down into a compound called methemoglobin. It couldn't have come from the guy in the storage room if it was still bright red."

"Look at you being all helpful and stuff."

I got a smirk and a response so dry it sucked the moisture from the air. "Don't get too excited. We could be looking at a combination of both men's blood with Milo's injuries going untreated and keeping the whole thing fresh."

Pin, meet the balloon of my hopes.

"I guess."

With that cheery thought in my head, I excused myself and went to the kitchen to beg for sustenance, only to find I'd arrived during Jason's break between breakfast and lunch. The place was deserted. Too tired to wait around, I backtracked and went home to finally take that nap.

CHAPTER EIGHT

It felt like my head had barely touched my pillow when my phone rang, but I'd been out for a solid four hours, and it was still shy of dinnertime.

"Hello." The word grated from my sandpaper throat. If it hadn't been the day before a planned event, I'd have tapped the ignore button, let Martha Tipton suck it up, and gone back to sleep.

"You sound awful," Martha's voice hit my ear as more shrill than usual. I winced.

"Thanks," I said but didn't ask what she wanted. Maybe Martha would take the hint. And perhaps a dragon would fly out of her butt and take me for a ride.

Then again, I had to ask myself, did I really want to ride Martha's butt dragon?

Probably not. Clearly, I needed more sleep.

"What can I do for you, Martha? I've had a pretty long day as it is." Or more like three long days rolled into one.

"It's just that I...it's...well, strange things have been happening." That last bit came out all in a rush. "I'm in the storage shed. Can you come?"

Hadn't she brushed me off mere hours before?

"What kinds of strange things?"

"It's...you wouldn't believe me if I told you. Can you just come and see?"

Strange, unexplainable things? Sounded like Davina hadn't wasted any time making good on her promise.

"I suppose." I tried to suppress a sigh and was almost successful.

"It's fine," Martha clipped the words, her tone going hard. "Never mind." She hung up. Two warring impulses rose within me. The first to take her at her word, the second to haul myself out of bed, go over there, and give her a piece of my mind. Maybe not a big piece since it was a sleep-addled hornet's nest in there.

But, of course, just thinking about the various options cued up enough brain cells to keep me from going back to sleep, so I went with the second, but with the addition of a stop for coffee on the way.

The front parking lot was empty, so I pulled around back to check for Martha. I found her near the former bus garage converted into a storage unit when the elementary school became the town office. If she'd woken me out of a sound sleep and then left, I was in the mood to show up on her doorstep and air my grievances, so it was good that her car still sat near the rolled-up door.

It wasn't good that Martha leaned against the hood, staring into the opening. Her eyes were wide and dazed when she turned to look at me. "We've been vandalized."

What we'd been was Davina'd. This mess had the

mark of ghost written all over it. Halloween had come to the storage unit a day early, and I had to admit, Davina had done a bang-up job of getting her point across.

"How many bags of fake cobwebs do you think that is?"

I stared wonderingly at the festoon of polyester filament stretched from side to side, front to back, and floor to ceiling, forming an impenetrable web peppered with plastic spiders.

"Comes in a case of twelve," Martha said.

"And how many cases were in here?" I didn't expect an answer to the dry question.

"Just the one." Martha's ability to process sarcasm could use some work.

Having used a single bag of the stuff the year before, and there still being a few strands stuck in my rose-bushes, my first instinct was to yell "not it" and run away. To be honest, escape was my second instinct as well.

Hands on her hips, Martha surveyed the damage. "Who would do a thing like this?"

I knew the answer to that one, but it fell into the realm of stranger than fiction, so I shrugged and tried to decide the best plan of attack for cleaning up the mess.

"Whoever it was is on my list," I said slightly more loudly than the space between us warranted. If Davina was hovering anywhere within hearing distance, I wanted her to know there would be repercussions. What those might be, I had no idea. What was I going to do to her that could be worse than death?

Exactly nothing. That's what. And Davina knew it. Where was that Ghostbusters trap thingie when you needed it? Anything I could use as a bargaining chip would be helpful.

But standing around lamenting over a hot mess doesn't get it cleaned up, and while this was something Martha brought on herself, she didn't know that, so I felt obligated to help.

"You got any tools around here? We need scissors, or better yet, a good, sharp pair of garden shears. Unless you've got a machete just, you know, lying around." Not that I expected Martha to pull one of those out of her pocket.

"There's a nice pair of secateurs I keep on hand for dead-heading the roses and harvesting the hips."

Things were looking up. "Great. Where? I'll grab them, and if I can manage with one hand, I'll get started. If not, you'll have to call someone else to help." I turned toward the office, but Martha's next sentence stopped me cold.

"They're hanging on the pegboard at the back of the storage unit."

Wonderful.

I sighed and internally cursed Davina to an eternity of hearing only one song...The Macarena. Probably wouldn't take, but a girl could hope, right?

"Oh!" Martha perked up. "Wait right here. I have just

the thing." She bustled off toward the town office. I called for Davina while she was gone, but the ghost was smart enough not to show her face. A few moments later, Martha returned, her face alight with excitement and holding a sheathed sword.

"This has been kicking around in the storage closet since we took over the old school and before that when we had the town office in the back room of the grange hall. Do you think it will work?"

She held the sheath while I drew the sword, which appeared sharp enough to hurt myself since I was doing everything one-handed. "I guess we'll see." Moving forward, I began to hack away at the strands of polyester. The sword was sharp enough, and Davina's hubris helped me in the end. She'd strung the web tightly to make it more difficult for anyone to get through the mess, but the tautness allowed for easier cutting.

As I hacked and slashed, Martha went behind me and stripped the loosened fluff from its anchor points. We didn't get it all by any means but cleared enough to allow access to the stacks of tarps and the wooden frames that would later hold them.

"It's a good thing I didn't wait until the set-up crew showed up. I'd hate for anyone to have to deal with this," Martha said.

"Except for me, you mean." Again, the sarcasm was lost on her.

"Next town meeting, I'm putting in a recommendation for some sort of surveillance system. I don't know what the world is coming to when people make mischief just for the sake of it. Probably kids, but even so."

"Mmmhp," was my answer. I knew better but couldn't tell her without yanking back the curtain on the existence of ghosts and that I could see them—my deepest secret. And yet, my entire being yearned to call her out for the stupid thing she'd done to bring on the wrath of Davina.

I felt like I'd hit half past midnight on day three of a two-day bender. My ears buzzed, my tongue was fuzzy, and I wasn't sure I could trust my thoughts not to fall out of my mouth without benefit of a trip past my brain first.

"If that's everything, I've had a long day already, and it's time for my painkillers." I waved my wrapped wrist in her face. "I'll be back first thing in the morning."

Now that I'd fixed the problem for her, Martha was happy as a clam. My errant brain tried to determine if it knew who'd decided clams were happy and failed. She waved me off, and I didn't argue.

CHAPTER NINE

Drew hammered the last tent peg into the ground, tied a complicated knot around it, then tested the line for tautness. The orange tarp bounced slightly but seemed solid enough and fit for purpose.

"Sorry, babe. I didn't plan on dragging you into this mess." He'd taken the day off to help with the event set-up since my wrist put me out of commission.

"No worries." Bending, he dropped a kiss on my cheek. "As a local business owner, it's my civic duty to get involved in community affairs."

"That sounds like a phrase Martha would use to guilt a person into participating."

He grinned. "Who said she didn't? She's right, and besides, I'm looking forward to putting on my Thor costume and handing out candy later. I love Halloween."

So was I, come to that. Not looking forward to handing out candy but to seeing Drew in his Thor costume.

"You wear that tonight, and I'll make sure you get some sugar once the Trick or Treaters have all gone home."

His second kiss landed on my lips and nearly blew the top of my head off when he leaned into it. "I'll bring my hammer."

"I'm counting on it."

I might have kept the banter going if a scream hadn't sliced the air.

Martha. I'd know that shrill voice anywhere.

"What the..." Drew took off at a lope in the direction of the scream, leaving me in his dust. Running hurt my wrist, so I power-walked to keep the jarring to a minimum and arrived at the other end of the tarp labyrinth just in time to see him lift a limp Martha in his arms.

My heart skipped a beat, then pounded in my ears. "What happened? Is she bleeding?"

"I don't think so," he turned in place as if looking for somewhere to put her down. "Only fainted." Martha's head bobbled as he used his elbow to point toward the tarp wall to his left. "She was looking at something over there. Big spider, maybe, and then she just collapsed."

A betting woman might put money on the spider's name being Davina.

"There's a First Aid station over by the bait shop. Do you think you can carry her that far?"

"I am Thor. I am mighty." He shifted the limp body into a better position and headed for the closest exit.

"Mighty is one word for it," Davina's voice preceded the chill of her presence. I turned to see her watching

Drew's butt as he walked away. It was a nice butt, but she didn't need to point that out.

"What did you do?"

Not the least bit apologetic, Davina shrugged. "Nothing much. Martha's kind of a wimp for all her bluff and bluster."

"What. Did. You. Do?"

"I put my hand on the tarp. That's all."

Somehow, I doubted that.

My thousand-yard stare shook loose the rest of the story. "And said her name."

She cut her gaze away, so I knew there was more to it than that and waited her out.

"In a spooky voice."

"I have to go see if she's okay. Find something else to do." Turning my back on her, I stalked away. Honestly, these ghosts caused me nothing but trouble, and Davina was rapidly shaping up to be the worst of the lot. "And stay away from Martha for the rest of the day."

I'd gone a step too far. The air around me went cold enough to steal my breath. Ice crystals formed on the green coating of the tarp.

"I do what I want," Davina stated.

"Yeah, well, so do I. You want my help in moving onto the next plane of existence, you might want to consider being a bit less of a pain in my backside."

With that, I hugged myself against the chill and left her to consider what I said. She didn't have to know I was shaking on the inside from knowing how little effort on her part it would take to demolish the entire morning's work of setting up the event.

I met Drew on his way back.

"Martha?" I asked as he reversed direction and fell into step beside me.

"Awake, annoyed there's no one on duty to dance attendance on her and asking for you." He put a hand on my elbow to guide me toward the First Aid station. "She's got quite a story to tell."

"I've already heard it," I kept my voice low in case anyone was nearby. "From the guilty party."

He gave me a puzzled look, and I sighed.

"It's a long story, but here are the salient points: Davina has a lookalike. Martha found the lookalike and hired her to haunt the Halloween event for publicity purposes. Davina took offense and decided turnabout was fair play, so she's been haunting Martha."

"Intentional karma," he said.

"If intentional karma is another word for payback, then yeah, I guess that's accurate enough." I sighed. "But I don't think it follows the spirit of the concept even if Martha was the one who gave the karma ball a push to get it rolling."

"Never a dull moment in Everly's world." If his voice hadn't held a touch of admiration, he'd have suffered an elbow to the ribs. Or maybe I'd have sicced Davina on him. "I'll just go find something productive to do, okay?

There were more tent stakes to pound with my mighty hammer.”

A little Martha goes a long way. “Chicken.”

He’d already turned to leave, so the low-voiced chicken noises barely drifted back.

Men.

I ducked into the tent.

“Oh, Everly. There you are.” Prone, on something that looked like a stretcher and a camp bed had a baby, Martha rested the back of her hand on her forehead, closed her eyes, and took a deep, dramatic breath.

At least with her eyes closed, she didn’t see me rolling mine.

“Are you all right?” She did look a bit pale. Fear will do that to you.

“You’ll have to take over for me. I don’t see how I can go on after what just happened.”

Outside the tent, someone made a squeaking sound.

I raised my voice on a hunch, “You might as well come in, Delilah. I know all about your haunting scheme.”

The revelation put a little color back on Martha’s face. More than a little, actually. Flushed with guilt, she looked away. “I have no idea what you’re talking about.”

If my wrist had allowed, I’d have fisted hands on my hips and given her my best impression of my mother’s you’ve-been-naughty look. I had to settle for just the look.

“You can quit with the innocent act because I’m not buying a ticket to that particular show. You hired Delilah

Cannon to play Davina's ghost, then you altered the map of the tarp maze to make it easier for her to flit around in the background unseen."

"She didn't think anyone would notice," Davina observed in a dry tone as she popped into the space next to me.

"No one was supposed to notice," Martha confirmed Davina's suspicions as a woman wearing a floppy hat to hide her face sidled in through the tent door.

"Delilah, I presume." Hand out, I approached the woman. "I'm Everly Dupree, the coordinator for this little shindig."

"Oh." The hat came off. "I thought—" Her voice pitched low to match Davina's, the newcomer turned toward Martha for backup but got left to swing in the breeze.

Up close, Delilah's resemblance to Davina could not be denied. Her eyes sat a bit wider apart, her nose was slightly longer, and she'd used lip liner to alter the shape of her mouth subtly. From a distance, she'd be a dead ringer. No wonder Davina was annoyed.

"Martha heads up the committee for these town functions but mostly leaves the details to me."

"Dumps them on you, more like," Davina muttered. I could not disagree.

"Which is why," I continued as if I hadn't been interrupted. "I'm surprised to find you lurking about in this furtive manner."

Head swiveling, Delilah looked from me to Martha, then back again. "She didn't tell you about me."

"Not a peep."

"Well then." Delilah tossed the floppy hat down on the folding chair next to where Martha still lay, reached up, and gave a tug. When a wig joined the hat to reveal a mouse-brown head of hair under the blond, Davina let out a choked sound. "I guess that's the end of that." Delilah's true voice had a bit of a Betty Boop lilt. "It was time to move on anyway. I mean, really, what kind of psychic goes and lets herself get murdered like that? She really should have seen the danger coming."

The chill in the air didn't seem to register with Martha or Delilah.

Delilah spit on her own sleeve and rubbed the wet spot over her lips to leave a red blotch on the blue cloth and her mouth bare of artifice. She scanned the tent, helped herself to a pack of gauze and a squirt from a bottle of eye wash, then removed the skillful makeup that created subtle contours around her nose and eyes.

I shivered as the temperature dropped another few degrees. The smart thing would have been to just leave the tent and let Martha and Delilah hash things out on their own. Wild horses couldn't have dragged me away. I wanted to see what happened next.

So, apparently, did Davina. Scowling, she stood silent while, with no mirror and a practiced hand, Delilah plucked a blue contact from her left eye and flicked it on the ground. The right one followed.

"I won't be returning your payment, Martha. I'm sure we can both agree I've earned every penny."

No one watching the woman leave the First Aid tent would have pegged her as Davina Benet. Maybe as Davina's daughter or younger sister since she'd taken what looked like twenty years off her face with the makeup and her bone structure still carried a certain similarity. I'm not the best judge of these things, but my guess would put her at thirty-five, give or take a year.

"Well, I never," Martha took umbrage.

"I think we can both agree you had that coming. In fact, I think we can both agree you deserved worse. Can I have your word that there will be no more shenanigans?" That last was for Davina as much as Martha. I pinned the ghost with a look.

"We would have raised more money with a genuine ghost sighting on the agenda."

"I could still make that happen," Davina growled. "If that's what she really wants." But the air temperature had returned to something close to normal, so I figured it was safe to say no. Which I did. With emphasis.

"After your reaction to a harmless bit of haunting, I'd expect you to see the error of your ways. This is supposed to be a fun family event, not one that will send the kiddies home with nightmares. Let's keep it that way, shall we?

Are you feeling well enough to go back to work, or should I ask Drew to see you safely home?"

Still needing to talk to Delilah if I could catch her before she left, I hoped Martha would suck it up for once.

"I'm fine," Martha said, but if looks could kill, I'd have been the one haunting the littles at the end of the day. "No need to bother Drew while he's working so hard to get things ready." If her tone implied I hadn't been working, I decided to let it go and consider the crisis averted.

If I was lucky, this would be the worst thing to happen during the event.

I knew I'd jinxed myself the minute that thought crossed my mind.

CHAPTER TEN

"Hey, Delilah!" My wrist throbbed as I raced in front of her car just as she dropped it in drive and made ready to pull out of the parking space. "You got a minute?"

One look at her tear-stained face, and I regretted the impulse that had me chasing her down, but she nodded, took the car out of gear, and unlocked the doors. Taking the hint, I slid into the passenger seat.

"I'm sorry for how that all went down back there," I said. "I didn't mean to hurt your feelings or anything."

"It's not that." Delilah reached across me to pull a pack of tissues from the glove box. She took one and handed me the rest. "This world is so empty without Davina in it."

Crap. She'd made it seem like she was over the whole Davina thing. Wasn't that just two minutes ago?

"I don't know how I can be expected to go on without her."

Apparently not.

"I truly am sorry for your loss." From what the ghost

had told me, the two women hadn't been close enough for this level of despair. "How well did you know Davina?"

"She was my best friend, my reason for living. We had a connection, an instant bond right from the first time we met. I know she felt it, too."

Not according to her, but okay. To keep Delilah talking, I nodded and handed her another tissue.

"Where did you and Davina meet?" I'd already heard the story from one side. It couldn't hurt to get it from the other.

Delilah honked into her tissue, demanded another—the last in the pack—and dabbed her eyes dry before she began her tale.

"I'm originally from Haverhill," she said as if that should explain everything.

"Okay." I didn't get it.

"Haverhill. Massachusetts."

The same response sprang to my lips, but I bit it back and nodded as if I had a clue. I'd been through Haverhill once when some idiot cutting across lanes caused a pile-up on the 495. What little I remembered about the town was hazed over in a blur of listening to my ex complain about stupid drivers the rest of the way to Andover.

"Tell me more." Seemed a safe enough response, and it worked.

"Angeline Kowalski had been missing for two days before Davina showed up to solve the case."

"Right."

The name triggered a flood of information. I'd read about the Kowalski case in my research on Davina. While her parents slept, the four-year-old had climbed out her bedroom window to chase after a kitten she'd seen wandering loose.

"The police had begun to suspect foul play and were looking hard at the family, but there was this one detective who believed the parents were innocent and called in Davina. I was twelve or thirteen at the time." Delilah verified my age math. "I will never forget it. She was like an avenging angel, marching down the sidewalk with a trail of cops behind her. You've never seen anything like it."

"They found the little girl in someone's backyard, right?"

Delilah nodded. "Two houses down from mine. She figured her mother wouldn't let her keep the kitten, so she carried it almost a mile and hid in an old plastic playhouse. No one thought she could walk that far, so nobody looked in my neighborhood, but Davina knew."

No doubt, but I'd put good money on the fact she didn't know that was when she'd sparked Delilah's interest. The question now was, how deep did that interest go? Deep enough for murder, or maybe for stalking, in which case, she might have some useful information.

"Since you attended so many tapings, maybe you can help me out. Do you know of anyone who held a grudge against Davina? Anyone who would want to hurt her?"

I didn't even get the sentence out before Delilah began

shaking her head. "No one. Everyone loved her. Don't you see? She was an angel sent to this earth to help the lost find their way home, and when it was her time, the heavens called her back."

It had been a long weekend already, and I probably could have chosen my words more carefully, but I didn't. "Seems like if the heavens wanted her back, they could have found a less brutal way of making it happen. Dying in her sleep springs to mind."

Cue more tears and also a look designed to send me to the beyond.

"If you think of anyone or remember anything that might help, could you let me know?" I would probably regret it later, but I also offered to listen if she needed to talk about her loss, but the offer worked. Delilah handed me her cell phone, so I could add my name and number to her contacts list. "I'd like to see Davina get justice, so no detail is too small. You can text or call anytime."

I returned her phone, got out, and watched her drive away, thinking I'd never hear from her again. I should have known better.

CHAPTER ELEVEN

*P*utting murder out of my head for the moment, I took a final tour of the event setup, stopping at the booth where my father and mother would sell apple cider donuts and coffee to raise money for the high school's winter musical.

"I'll take two of those and a cup of coffee." The air smelled of sugar and cinnamon. "Better make that three. Drew has a sweet tooth."

Before she filled my order, my mother leaned out and gave me an up and down look. "How's the wrist? Any pain? You haven't been overdoing it, have you?"

"I'm fine, Mom. Honest. Drew did all the heavy lifting. He's worse than you are when it comes to coddling unless it's during self-defense class, so you don't have to worry. Once I'm healed up, you should come to class with me."

Still, my dad ducked out the back of the booth and came around to give me one of his hugs. Those things really should be patented. For the half a minute that it lasted, I leaned in and let his solid presence wash away every ounce of stress.

"Your mom's just a mom. They worry you know," he whispered, his fake mustache tickling my ear.

"Thanks, I needed that." Stretching to tiptoes, I kissed his cheek, and when he went back into the booth, I followed to give my mom a hug as well.

"I really am okay, and I have to get back to my final walk-through. Then I plan to sneak into the shop, put on my costume, and enjoy the festivities. You guys look cute, by the way. Miss Marple and Hercule Poirot, right? Very literary. Love the mustache."

"Naturally," my mother grinned. "He wants to grow his own now, but I had to put my foot down."

My father nailed the accent. "It's very dapper, n'est ce pas?"

"Quite. I assume you'll forgo the up-and-over hairstyle." I patted him on the cheek and ducked back into the labyrinth since it stood between the school booth and the fitness center. Two left turns, and a right would take me where I wanted to go.

Or it would have if Martha hadn't screwed around with the layout. Instead, I came out in front of Patrea's office, spotted Jober Peavey sitting on the steps, and in my haste to get to him, nearly ran over Bess Tate, who hovered just to the left of the exit and wore, I kid you not, a pink ladies costume from Grease. When I looked back, Jober had gone. Just my luck.

"Sorry, Bess, or is that Rizzo? I didn't see you there. Everything okay?" She'd missed the last couple of planning meetings because her nephew and his family had come up to visit for a week.

"Whose big idea was this?" She waved to indicate, I assumed, the altered layout of the maze. "Yours or Martha's? I thought I was near the bait shop but ended up here."

"It wasn't mine. Did you have a good visit with your family?"

Changing the subject put a wide smile on her lined face, brightening her whole complexion since she idled at sour most of the time. When she pulled out a new cell phone to show me pictures, I realized I'd hit the proud auntie button.

"Nathan bought me a new phone with a fancy schmancy camera so I can video chat with the kids, and we took selfies."

Lots and lots of selfies. I swiped through a solid dozen until I noticed one taken close to the spot where we currently stood. "Hey, that's Patrea in the background. If she'd have looked up, we'd call that a photobomb."

Bess frowned, so I explained the concept. "Oh," she said. "It's like Killroy was here."

Then she had to explain Killroy to me. While she did, I felt a tingle at the back of my neck. Not the kind I get from ghosts, but the kind I get when something significant is about to happen. Momma Wade says it's my spirit guide giving me a poke to make sure I pay attention.

Whatever it was, I tapped the photo to check the

time/date stamp, and my neck tingle paid off. "Bess," I held out the phone. "Is this right? The date and time, I mean. This was taken the day Davina Benet died, right? Right after the protest."

"You mean the most talked-about, gossip-worthy event in months, and I missed it by minutes because Martha Tipton wanted to hog the spotlight and didn't bother to tell me? Yes, thank you for the reminder."

Mooselick River ran on gossip, and Bess Tate certainly did her part to stay at the center of the hub. For once, that worked in my favor.

If I wasn't hampered by a broken wrist, I'd have picked her up and whirled her around. As it was, I leaned over and kissed her right on the lips. At any other time, I'd have enjoyed how her expression went from confused to suspicious and back to confused.

"You have to take this to the police station and show it to Ernie." While I had her phone in my hand, I sent myself a copy of the clearest photo, just for insurance.

"Why would I want to do a thing like that? He's seen Nathan and his family before."

My heart sang. "Because unless he's an absolute moron, he'll have to drop the charges against Patrea. She can't have been murdering Davina at the exact same time she was sitting at her desk, now, can she?"

"Oh!" Bess's mouth rounded, her eyes going sharp as she contemplated becoming the harbinger of justice. "I suppose not, and you think showing these photos to Ernie will help?"

"I do. Would you like me to go with you?" Not that my presence would be overly helpful, given Ernie's current mood when it came to me.

Bess shook her head and carefully placed her phone back in the pink patent leather handbag that matched her satin jacket. "Nathan's around here somewhere. He'll go with me."

"That's good, and Bess, I think this might be one of those times where it's best to hold our cards close to the vest until we know the outcome. There are already enough rumors going around about Patrea as it is. Can you promise to keep this just between us until we know whether it's enough to get the charges dropped?"

"As in, you won't say anything to Martha so I can get one up on her?"

I mimed the zipper across my mouth. "My lips are sealed."

Bess repeated the gesture. "Sold," she said. "I'll go right now. I'd like to get back in time for the costume contest." Moving faster than I'd have given her credit for, she spun until her skirt whirled up. "I think I have a shot at a prize this year."

"Well, you've got my vote," I said to her retreating back.

Lighter of heart than I'd felt since Friday, I tucked

away the knowledge of what might be and headed over to Jacy and Neena's shop, Curated Collections, to change into my costume and enjoy the rest of the event.

CHAPTER TWELVE

*M*onday dawned in a wash of dismal gray fog under an equally dismal gray sky. The day suited my mood right down to the ground, so I dressed in somber colors to match and let Drew help wrangle my hair into a messy bun. Not because I'd been shooting for the messy-bun look, but because that was the extent of his expertise with pins and coated elastic bands.

Even if Ernie released Patrea, I still had two ghosts on my hands, no leads, no new clues, and the least cooperative victims that ever lived, or in this case, died. Ghosts are not permitted to discuss the details surrounding their deaths, which would have made my life much easier. Oddjob wouldn't come near me, and Davina wasn't telling me much about how she'd lived. If something didn't shake loose soon, I'd have to consider taking desperate measures. Not that I had any real idea what those might be.

I hadn't solved Davina's murder over the weekend, and I hadn't seen or heard from Bess since I'd sent her to show Ernie the photos, so it seemed that gambit had also failed. I needed to stop by the station to check in, but since it was the first of November, I had an office to open and rents to collect, which wouldn't take more than a couple of hours. I took Molly with me to the office, knowing little Jamie Anderson would look for her when his mother—one of few holdouts against electronic payments—came in to drop off her check.

When Leo Hanson hired me to manage his rental properties, I spent the first few months talking him into letting me set up alternate rental payment methods—a plan embraced wholeheartedly by the younger tenants and even a few older ones. I processed receipts for the online payments, opened envelopes with mailed checks, and looked through estimates for projected upgrades before Jane finally pulled up out front.

"Jamie's here, Molls," I told the dog, who responded with an excited wiggle and wag on the way to the door to wait for him. "You be gentle with him, okay? No jumping." Her tail thumped twice as if she understood, and probably she did.

"Everything going okay, Jane?" Cute as a button, young Jamie had recently developed a penchant for putting toys into any hole he could find, including sink drains and heat registers, which had caused us both no end of trouble. "No more toy soldiers doing a deep dive into the sink?"

Jane shook her head and grinned, and for the first time since I'd met her didn't look like she'd been picked up by a tornado and put back down in another county with a case of shell shock. She glanced at her son as he slung chubby arms around Molly's neck and turned his face to accept the swipe of a slobbery dog tongue across his cheek. The boy's giggles brought a smile to both our faces.

"She's so gentle with him." Jane sat down in the chair opposite my desk as much because there was something she wanted to talk to me about as to give her son more time for doggy kisses and cuddles.

"Molly's a lover." Getting a dog hadn't been part of my life plan, but I wouldn't trade her for anything now. "She's good company, sweet as the day is long, and loves kids." And doesn't bark much at ghosts—but I left that part off.

Somehow I didn't think Molly was what Jane wanted to talk about, and I was right.

"Is something wrong?" I prodded gently.

"Here's my rent check," Jane slipped an envelope marked rent from her purse and slid it across the table to me.

"Thanks," I moved the envelope to the side, clasped my hands on the desk, and waited. Finally, I said, "You look rested."

"My mom's been staying with me for a few weeks while her roof gets fixed. She's been a huge help with Jamie."

No wonder she looked like a new woman.

"How nice for you. Will it be a long visit?"

Jane shifted in her seat. "That's the thing. She's been

trying to get me to move in with her since my dad passed away."

If memory served, Jane's lease had another three months to go, but Leo wouldn't penalize her for needing to break it so long as she gave thirty days' notice. But when I told Jane as much, the smile fell off her face, and she shook her head violently.

"No. I don't want to give notice. My mom's place needs more work than she can afford. With dad gone, she's let too many things go. Leo keeps my rental in such great shape we decided it would be better if she sold the house and moved in with me. I was hoping I could add her to the lease."

Inwardly, I sighed in relief. The absolute worst part of my job was interviewing potential tenants. "Sure. We can add her to the lease anytime. She'll need to bring some ID and sign some papers."

Jane's sigh wasn't inward at all. "Thank you. That's such a relief, and with both of us there, we can afford to pay more if we have to."

I shook my head. "You won't. That's not how Leo does things, and since he might be interested, do you mind telling me where your mom's house is and how much she'll be asking? If the price is right, he might want to buy it off her directly. Save you the cost of hiring an agent."

Every last ounce of tension slid off Jane's shoulders. "That would be something." She gave me the relevant details, adding. "The place needs some TLC. Those old gingerbread houses usually do, and it's been way too big for her for quite a while now, so it may need more work than it's worth. That's what the handyman who worked on the roof told her."

"Handyman?" Could it be?

"Yeah." Jane's smile dimmed. "That guy who died over the weekend. I guess we'll have to find someone to finish the job if Leo doesn't buy the place."

"We'll see." I smiled. "I'll talk to him and let you know."

"Thanks, Everly. I feel so much better. With my mom around to help more, I've re-enrolled at the University in Augusta. I only had seven credit hours to finish my post-grad coursework and get my paralegal certification. I'd been hoping to get a job with that new lawyer in town, but I heard she was arrested for murder, so I guess my perfect job went out the window."

"I wouldn't be too hasty with that decision." So long as Bess Tate came through, Patrea would be back in business in no time.

We chatted a while longer and made an appointment for her mother to come in and sign the lease.

CHAPTER THIRTEEN

O n the way home, I breezed into the back door of the shop Jacy and Neena owned together. Half second-hand shop with an eclectic mix of antiques and second-hand items, the other half, an art gallery where Neena showed her work and that of several other artists, Curated Collections did a brisk business most of the year.

"I'll just get them for you," Jacy spoke over her shoulder as she nipped into the back room to retrieve a box of books from the office. "Hey," she said to me when she saw me.

"Barb's bodice rippers?" The thought of Barbara Dexter reading about heaving cleavage and throbbing manhood always made me smile. I followed Jacy into the office.

"If you think that's funny, wait until I tell you where this batch came from." She waggled her eyebrows and grabbed what she'd come for. "Biggest bunch yet, too."

"Color me intrigued." I might not be as fully plugged into the gossip network as Jacy, but I did like a juicy tidbit every now and then. Trying to think who might be the mystery purveyor of racy books, I followed Jacy to the front of the shop.

"Hey, Barb. Long time, no see. How have you been?" You couldn't say we'd formed a fast friendship, but when you've been through the process of finding and dealing with a dead body with someone, it creates a bond.

"Just the person I wanted to see," she responded with a warm but slightly feral smile that I took, rightly so, as a warning she wanted something from me that I might not want to give. "I'm in a bit of a pickle and could use your help."

Since the last time I'd given Barbara a hand had involved cleaning up the next best thing to toxic waste, I decided to respectfully decline. "I'm sorry," I held up my injured arm so she could see the cast on my wrist. "I won't be able to go on housekeeping duty for a few more weeks."

The feral smile widened. "It's a good thing I don't need a housekeeper, then, isn't it? I need you to run the motel for me for a couple of days so I can fly out to watch my new grandson come into the world."

How could I say no to that?

"When do you need me?"

"Not until next Thursday. Should give you plenty of time to get ready." The matter settled, Barbara paid for her box of sexy romances and headed for the door, began to push through, then turned back.

"Shame about Jober Peavey. I hear you were the one

who found him." Her tone went up at the end, edging the statement toward a question.

"It wasn't just me, but yes, you heard right."

"Can't say I'm surprised," Barbara shuffled the box into a more comfortable position and took a step back from the door.

"It's not like I go looking for bodies, you know." My mother warned me about things I should avoid if I didn't want to get a reputation in high school. I didn't think I'd end up having to apply that concept to my adult life or in this context.

"I didn't mean you. I meant that someone took old Jober out of the picture."

Quiet up to now, Neena asked the question we were all thinking. "Why?" The three of us exchanged a quick glance. Here was our chance to maybe learn something helpful.

Taking another step back from the door, Barbara set the box of books on the floor and fisted hands on her hips. "Don't get me wrong, I liked Oddjob well enough, and I wouldn't want to speak ill of the dead."

The word *but* could have been a neon sign blinking over her head.

"But," Jacy prodded when the silence drew out long.

"But he was one of the most obnoxious men I have ever had the misfortune to meet, and I'm surprised someone hadn't done away with him before now." Barbara's eyes glittered with strong emotion.

My mouth dropped open at the amount of venom in her tone, and I heard Jacy mutter, "Tell us how you really feel."

Barbara returned to tell her tale of woe, leaving the box of books behind. "You combine a dirty mind, a vivid imagination, and a heaping dose of self-righteousness with a big, old gossipy mouth, you shouldn't be surprised to land your sorry backside in an early grave."

"Are we talking about someone who liked to gossip or someone who liked to threaten to gossip?" One of those could be an annoyance. The other ranked right up there on the list of possible motives for murder. Jober had threatened to out secrets on the night of his death. Maybe it hadn't been an isolated incident.

Barbara raised her left brow and gave me a nod. "I see you understand the distinction," she said.

"Are you thinking he blackmailed someone?" Neena propped her elbows on the counter, her gaze tracking over to rest briefly on the box of racy books.

Eyes alight, Barbara touched a finger to her nose before heading over to collect her box of books to leave. "I could be wrong, but people tend to forget themselves and talk about things they shouldn't when someone's been in their house awhile, and he was in and out of a great many houses in town. Now, he's dead. You do the math."

With that, she sailed out the door.

"Okay." Jacy came around from behind the counter as soon as Barbara had cleared the front steps. "I don't know about you, but I have thoughts." She led the way to the current furniture rotation near the shop window, settling on the short side of a sectional sofa I hadn't seen before.

Royal blue, crushed velvet, somewhat boxy shape, quilted back, with rhinestone studs along the base and clear legs meant to look like crystal. It was both gaudy and sublime. Everything my ex would have hated.

I had to have it.

"This sold?" The sofa accepted my backside as if the two had been fated to meet.

Jacy slowly shook her head. "Just came in this morning. There's a matching chair, too."

"Consider it mine, then. I'll cut you a check before I leave, and I'll have Drew round up the guys to pick it up. It would go great in the front room my mother calls a parlor."

Behind me, Neena snickered.

"What?" I whirled to catch her with her hand over her mouth.

"Nothing," she lied right to my face, but I had no way to prove it. "I think it's high time you added a few more personal touches to your place."

Eyes narrowed, I glanced at Jacy, who managed to keep whatever she felt from showing on her face. If I had to guess, I'd say they'd engaged in a friendly wager on whether I'd want the sofa, but since I knew they loved me, I let it go.

"Back to my thoughts," Jacy said. "I doubt Barbara

murdered Oddjob for discovering her steamy novel collection—or that she'd have brought it up if she had—but if he'd been going around town blackmailing people, I'm not surprised he's dead."

I nodded. "We all heard him threaten to reveal several secrets in the bar, so I wouldn't call the theory a stretch."

"Given the timing, I'd say we narrow our pool of suspects to people who were there that night. We can widen out from there if we have to." Neena picked some white fuzz from the arm of the sofa, shook her fingers to dislodge the fluff, then narrowed her eyes when static made it stick.

Rising, Jacy retrieved a pen and a spiral notebook from behind the counter and returned to her spot. "From where I stood, I thought he pointed toward Jenny Sandler, but it could have been Bennie, the mechanic, too. They were both at the bar."

"Together?"

"No. Bennie's married, and so's Jenny, I think. Be pretty ballsy of them to show up at Cappy's together if anything is going on. Plus, I can't see her unbending enough to crawl into bed with Bad Boy Bennie," Jacy said. "Not that anyone calls him that anymore. He's cleaned up his act since he opened the garage."

Neena frowned, her face going a bit stormy. "He was one of Hudson's gambling buddies, so maybe his halo isn't quite so polished as you think."

Despite her making the odd bet with Jacy, Neena's

husband's gambling was a sore spot. If he'd kept his wallet in his pocket, he might not have been staying at the Bide-A-Way at the time of his murder, and maybe she wouldn't have missed out on a portion of his final days. I could see why that might make her bitter. They'd been in the process of reconciling, but that decision had come just a little too late.

Hudson hadn't held the separation against his wife, and I would know since he'd been my first ghost and told me so.

I closed my eyes for a second to try pulling up a clearer mental image of the bar from that night.

"Wasn't there a man sitting between Jenny and Ben anyway? My memory is a little hazy, and I don't know what her husband looks like, so it could have been him. To be honest, neither of them rings the killer bell for me, but we'll keep them on the list along with Thea Lombardi's entire table." I nodded to indicate Jacy should write it down. "So that's Thea, Jason from the Marlow, and the Campbells—Nelson and Darcy."

Jacy shook her head, then pointed the pencil at me. "

Troubled, Neena rubbed the spot between her eyes. "If we're makin' lists, I think we have to leave Milo on there. He was behind the bar, and Miranda, too."

"I suppose." Jacy jotted down the names and added one more. "And Adam, the cook as well. What's the plan? Corner these people and demand they tell us their dirty secrets?"

"You could get out the rubber hose and beat the truth out of them."

None of us had heard Patrea come in through the back. Her mile-wide grin lightened the mood considerably as we all jumped up to offer hugs.

"How did you get out?" Neena asked. I'd forgotten to mention Bess and her selfie-defense.

At the same time, Jacy wanted to know, "Did you get an early bail hearing?"

She held up a hand to stop the barrage of questions. "Nope. I'm sprung. Alibied out."

"Bess came through?" I asked, and Patrea nodded.

Jacy went behind the counter, grabbed Patrea a bottle of water from the mini-fridge, handed it over, and settled back in her spot on the sofa. "I feel like I've come in at the end of a movie. What did Bess do?"

"This is nice." Once she'd picked a spot, Patrea brushed a hand over the seat. "You should get this, Everly. It would make a great centerpiece for that front room of yours."

"Does everyone think I need to redecorate?"

In a good mood, Patrea grinned. "And remove the overwhelming essence of old lady from the decor? Never."

"It's not that bad, and I already bought the sofa," I said with a neener-neener vibe. "Plus the matching chair."

Jacy waved a hand. "That's old news. Now, spill! How did you get alibied out?"

Long legs crossed, Patrea leaned back. "Bess Tate

showed up at the station yesterday afternoon with her nephew and her cell phone. It seems the whole family had posed for a selfie outside my office right around the time of Davina's death. With the time and date stamp and taken at the perfect angle for a great shot through my front window showing me plainly visible sitting at my desk. He had to call in someone from IT to verify that it was legit, but once they did, it was enough for Ernie to let me go."

"That must have stuck in his craw," Neena reached over to give Patrea's hand a squeeze.

"He apologized quite nicely. Probably afraid I'd sue his pants off, but either way, I am officially off the hook for murder."

"That's one down," Jacy said, licking her finger and drawing a mark in the air, "one to go."

"You mean Milo and the unfortunate death at Cappy's? I've got some inside scoop in that." Patrea leaned forward. "Milo's still in the hospital. Or he was when I left the station this morning. Severe concussion. I think I heard Ernie call it a grade three, and there was some mention of a hairline skull fracture."

The mood in the shop lost all sense of light-heartedness.

"Sounds like he's lucky to be alive." Neena shuddered. "And it sounds like he was another intended victim, not the killer."

"Highly possible. Or else he walked in at the wrong

time, and the killer had to do something. The angle and placement of the injury were consistent with an attack from behind. He was hit with something round, like a baseball bat or a pipe." Patrea grinned. "Ernie talks to himself when he types up reports, so I got to hear most of what went into that one."

If I closed my eyes, I could picture the scene and at least two possibilities for how it all went down. "The way I see it, Milo either walked in on the crime as it happened, and the killer wanted to shut him up."

"Oh!" Jacy sucked in a breath. "That's bad."

"Or he was in the way and had to be handled before the fact."

We all shuddered. "That's worse," Jacy said.

"No," I disagreed. "It would have been better if the killer knew for a fact he didn't see anything incriminating. But I think the truth lies somewhere in the middle because Milo said he saw a man's legs, which means he could still be in danger."

"Did Ernie mention any other suspects in his ramblings?" I turned to Patrea, who shook her head slowly.

Brightening slightly, Jacy said, "At least I think we can all agree on the motive."

"What motive?"

I'd forgotten Patrea had already been escorted from the bar when Oddjob went off on the verbal tangent that probably got him killed, so we all took turns filling her in on the chain of events.

"We were just making a list of suspects when you came in." Jacy turned the notebook so Patrea could see the list, then smirked when Patrea grabbed it for a closer look. "I think we should split up the list and see if we can narrow it down."

"I'll take Bennie. Old Sally's due for an oil change anyway, and I want him to give her a good going over. I've decided to upgrade, and I want to give the Buick to my dad. He loves that car, and he's got a milestone birthday coming up. I think she'd make a fine gift."

Two sets of eyebrows shot up—Jacy's and Neena's. Since Patrea already knew about my recent change of fortune, it was probably time to fess up to the others. "What? I don't deserve a new car?"

"A new car and a new sofa in the same week?" Jacy shook her head. "It's not like you to be so impulsive with money."

"Come on." My face heated up, and I didn't need a mirror to know it had gone red. "I buy stuff sometimes, and the sofa isn't new. It's used, and I got it for a good price."

"Nope." Neena tilted her head. "Something's up with you. Did Catherine have a cache of uncut diamonds squirreled away in her dresser drawers?"

I laughed at the absurdity, then had to admit to myself that it wouldn't have been beyond the realm of possibility.

A secret hoarder, the former owner of my house, had been a collector of…well…just about anything. Providing Jacy with enough items to stock the opening of this second-hand shop hadn't made much of a dent in the volume of stuff stored away in every nook and cranny of my house.

"Not so far, but I wouldn't rule anything out when it comes to Catherine." I took a deep breath. "Something else happened a week or so ago, and I haven't said anything because I wasn't sure what I wanted to do about it."

I told them about Tippy's trust expecting hurt feelings that I'd been hiding something from them, but these were my soul sisters, and I should have known better.

"That's fantastic. I assume Patrea has advised you to invest some of it." Jacy looked at Patrea, who nodded. "Then you'll buy that new car, but if I know you, you're already planning on doing something altruistic with most of the money because you don't think you earned it."

She had me pegged.

"Ding, ding." Patrea touched one index finger to her nose, pointed at Jacy with the other. "Give that girl a prize."

"It's a ridiculous amount of money," I muttered. "It feels dirty."

"That man turned your life upside down, nearly got you killed, and dragged your good name through the courts." Fired up, Neena waved her hands to emphasize her point. "Finding him buck-naked and chained to a bed might have been emotionally satisfying, but even jail was far less than he deserved. Take the money. Do things with it that make it feel clean and good, and consider that chapter of your life well over."

"You'll also need to adjust your will if you have one or draw one up if you don't. I can help you there." Patrea waggled a hand in my direction. "And you should probably pop in to talk to someone at the bank, so they know what's what. I assume you'll want to transfer the money from wherever Kitty opened the accounts to make things more convenient."

It was good advice and everything I'd planned to do anyhow. Their support for my decision came without a moment's consideration, which meant it came from their hearts, which touched mine. Uplifted, I fought back the sting of tears. I had a few ideas rolling around for what to do that would, as Neena had said, make me feel clean and good. But for now, there was a murder or two to solve.

"Thanks. I love you guys." Changing the subject, I reached over and took the list from Jacy. "I've got Bennie, and I can pop in and talk to Jason. I've promised to watch the desk for a few hours one day this week to give David a break."

"That leaves Jenny, Thea, Miranda, and the Campbells because I don't think we're getting anywhere near Milo right now," Jacy said. "I'll take Nelson Campbell because he just got a new job where Brian works, and they've been riding together. And if I run into Miranda, I know her well enough from filling in at Cappy's a few times when they needed help on a busy Saturday night that I'm sure she'll talk to me."

"I've got Darcy Campbell," Neena pointed her thumb toward the studio side of the shop. "She's been coming to my sip and paint classes, so I'll get her alone the first chance I get.

"Jenny's mine," Patrea said. "I have to talk to her about a building permit anyway because we're looking to expand the nursery side of the Christmas tree farm into something we can do year-round. Chris should have picked up the blueprints this morning but had to postpone for obvious reasons."

"Which leaves the dreaded Thea Lombardi." A moment of inspiration hit. "It's Monday, right? So you're closing soon anyway. Why don't we all head to the diner and celebrate Patrea's release from the hoosegow? My treat, and I'll even spring for pie."

With a wicked grin, Patrea clapped a hand over her heart. "I'm honored to be your excuse for getting out of talking to Thea Lombardi alone. But I hope they're not out of graham cracker pie."

CHAPTER FOURTEEN

Mabel poked her head out of the kitchen when she saw us come in. "Don't order off the menu. I've got something I want to try out on you." Her voice got some attention. On catching sight of Patrea, two older female customers turned away hastily, their mouths firming into disapproving lines. Fine, I thought. Be that way.

At least Thea was working, and the other two patrons had the decency to smile at us even if it was with naked curiosity written all over their faces.

"We're celebrating," Jacy spoke loudly enough for everyone in the place to hear. "We already knew Patrea was innocent, but now, Ernie has proof. Patrea wants graham cracker pie."

"I'll set a piece aside," Mabel offered. "And it's on the house. But I want your honest opinion on this new chicken sandwich."

One of the old biddies sniffed. Jacy sent her a stern look on her way past. The kind that lingered and made the woman look away as we settled into our favorite booth.

"What can I getcha to drink?" Thea looked bored as

usual, but that was just the way her face was made. Her eyes flicked toward Patrea, then studiously away.

"Sweet tea for me," Neena smiled up at Thea and got one of the server's patented head-to-toe appraisals. "The sweeter, the better, and don't you say a word about the calories. They don't count when it's a celebration."

"Whatever you need to tell yourself to get through the day," Thea said and rolled her eyes. Of all the possible suspects, she was the one I'd most like to see taken down a notch, but I still didn't think she was dumb enough to commit murder. Whether or not we could get her to spill her secrets was another story.

"Thea, would you bring me a piece of graham cracker pie," said one of the old biddies. "Please."

"There's only one left, and it's already spoken for," Thea didn't even look up. Someone should explain to her that the little niceties would go a long way toward increasing her tips.

"First come, first served, that's the rule." The tone was primarily proper, but the look that went along with it was full of venom.

Mabel popped up in the window between the kitchen and dining room. "This is my diner, and I make the rules. You'll have to choose something else. I'd recommend the caramel banana cream."

"That sounds good to me," I said. "Can you save a piece for me?"

"Sure thing," Mabel grinned at me, then said to the

customer trying to be difficult. "Sorry, I guess you'd better go for coconut or chocolate."

"I'm in for the coconut," Neena declared while Jacy claimed a piece of the chocolate.

"I suppose you're out of those now, too." The two older ladies decided they'd had enough. "Never mind. I've lost my appetite. If you could bring me the check, Thea."

She did, and they left in a huff.

"Sorry," I called back to the kitchen. "We didn't mean to cost you business."

"Pshaw." She waved a dismissive spatula. "It's always something with those two. They'll be back." Built for her former life in the roller derby, Mabel's tolerance for people who told her how to run her diner would fit in a Barbie shoe with room left over. And given her size, most people had the sense not to push the issue.

Four plates landed under the warming lights. Mabel disappeared for a moment, then reappeared at the door from the kitchen. She waved Thea off when the server went to pick up the plates and did it herself.

"This is grilled marinated chicken—my own recipe for the marinade—on a scratch-made brioche bun, with lettuce, grilled tomatoes, and my cold-packed, spicy pickles."

"If it tastes even half as good as it smells, you've got yourself a winner." My mouth had actually begun to water. I took the first bite, then groaned. "It does, and you do. This is fabulous."

The yummy noises from our table told the tale. "You need to have this on the menu. I'd order it at least once a week," Patrea decided. Mabel beamed at the praise. "Maybe twice."

Pleased, Mabel announced she was taking a break, went back to the kitchen while the last of the other customers paid, and left us alone with Thea.

Jacy winked at me, pitched her voice so Thea could hear. "Sure is a shame about Mr. Peavey. He was such a nice man."

"Jober Peavey was a cranky old fart and a crappy tipper with a filthy mind and no scruples." Thea collected a couple of nearly-empty ketchup bottles and set them on the counter for refilling. "I'm not saying he deserved to die, but the one thing he definitely wasn't was *nice*. I'm just calling it like it is."

"You're a good judge of character, and it sounds like you know more about him than we do." I laid it on thick. "Do you have any idea who might have wanted him dead?"

"Just about anyone he ever knew, probably." Returning, Thea leaned her butt against the table next to ours. "Thought he knew everything that went on in this town, but he didn't have a clue. I hear stuff. You can't work here without getting a good idea who's doing what...or who. People forget I'm here, and they talk. Mostly in snippets, but it's not hard to put things together."

Neena nodded and forced a smile. "They probably did

the same with him when he was doing his odd jobs in their homes."

"So he liked to make it seem. He tried his little game on me." More forthcoming than I'd expected her to be, Thea wrinkled her nose. "He thought he knew stuff. Well, I know stuff, too. Not too long before he and Leo fell out, Mabel hired Oddjob to clean the vent ducts. He skulked around here for three days listening to every little thing that was said. I even caught him in the office once, and I'm pretty sure he was going through the papers on the desk."

Because Jacy was Jacy, she rose, skirted gently past Thea, and refilled our drinks. She even brought Thea a glass of ice water.

"Was that why Leo went off on him?"

"No." To emphasize, Thea shook her head emphatically. "This happened before Mableo was a thing." The combination of Mabel and Leo's names struck me funny, but not as funny as Thea's next sentence. "Oddjob accused Leo of running a "house of ill repute" out of one of his rental houses."

Beside me, Jacy snorted. "He did not."

"He did, and then he got all kinds of pissed when Ernie didn't put down his roast beef sandwich and slap the cuffs on Leo right on the spot."

"What did Ernie say?" Patrea looked unamused, but I supposed Ernie wasn't her favorite person at the moment.

"Not a word." Smiling, and not in a nice way, Thea

returned to the counter to begin plating our pie. "Leo Hansen running hookers out of a rental house? I'm pretty sure we'll be putting out bird feeders for flying pigs before that ever happens. Anyone with half a brain knows better than to believe that. Ernie's a fool, but he's not a moron."

Her head turned just enough to keep Thea from being able to see her face, Patrea raised a brow and smirked.

"Anyhow." Thea went on. "Leo's wasn't even the craziest of Jober's stories that he ever told. He should have gotten a job writing for soap operas if he thinks Robin Thackery is in a cult."

My eyes went wide, and mine was not the only shocked expression at the table. Thea didn't seem to notice as she continued.

"And then, a couple of weeks ago, old Oddjob cornered me after his breakfast and said how he knew all my dirty secrets. Then he mentioned something he thought I wouldn't want made public. Didn't go off quite like he expected. Since I haven't done anything I'm ashamed of, I told him to piss up a rope."

Patrea shot up an eyebrow. "How did he take that?"

"You ever see a cat fall in water?" Thea actually smiled. Not the nicest smile, to be fair, but we'd set a record for how many times her lips turned up instead of down that day. "Lot of hissing and spitting. Mostly, it was like that."

So not too far off his performance at the bar.

"He had a pattern," Neena said quietly.

I nodded because she was right. "What was the price for his silence?" I almost felt sorry for Thea.

She looked at me like I'd just popped up fully formed from a pile of dung. "Nothing."

"He wasn't trying to blackmail you?"

"No." Thea's tone dripped with scorn. "I don't think so, anyway. It didn't feel so much like blackmail as just him wanting me to know he knew things. He said something about knowledge being power like he got off on it, if you know what I mean."

Her next statement made me choke on my lemonade.

"Man gets that concerned over everyone else's sex life probably doesn't have one of his own. Or else he had a teeny weenie and was overcompensating."

In all the time I'd known her, that had to be the biggest word I'd ever heard Thea use. And she probably wasn't wrong, but now, I knew whatever Oddjob had learned about her was related to relationships. Which led me to ask, "Are you and Jason an item?"

Okay, so she knew what it meant to overcompensate, but apparently, the word *item* tripped her up because her mouth dropped open and her forehead wrinkled as she tried to figure out what I meant.

"Dating. Are you and Jason dating?"

"If you call doing the wild thing dating, then I guess so."

Too. Much. Information. But I did ask, so I had only myself to blame. Someone kicked me under the table, and since Patrea was seated next to me, it had to be either Neena or Jacy. Given the laughter dancing in her eyes, I suspected Neena.

But I had to ask. "And were you...uh...doing the wild thing on Friday?"

Thea's answer cleared them both of murder and made me want to throw up in my mouth a little. Probably from the hip shimmy that went along with her statement. "All night long."

Patrea said, "Not much of a dirty secret. You're both full-grown adults."

"Who said banging Jason was my dirty secret?" With that, Thea left us to our own devices.

"Wasn't that fun?" I said when my mouth started working again. "And we have a new suspect to add to the list."

"Not it," Jacy said, then grinned when two of our lunch companions frowned.

"I'll talk to Robin." I gave in to the inevitable. "I've dealt with her enough to know how to get semi-valid information out of her."

"So," Neena picked up the last piece of her chicken sandwich and whispered. "Does that put Thea on the suspect list or take her off? I can't even tell at this point because I think my brain is broken."

I shook my head. "Me, either, but at least there's pie."

And it was good pie, too.

CHAPTER FIFTEEN

It wasn't that difficult to get Robin alone. Since I'd needed a few things, I cornered her coming out the grocery store's back door at the end of her shift.

"Hey," she said. "I haven't seen the dead psychic lately. Did you perform an exercise?"

I blinked. "Like working out?" Living with a fitness instructor had upped my game there, but it seemed like an odd question to ask.

"No, silly. An exercise." Her repeating the word as if I were stupid didn't help a bit, so I frowned, and she elaborated by miming holding up a cross with one hand and waggling the fingers of the other. "To cast out ghosts."

"I'm pretty sure you mean exorcism, and that's for demons, so the answer would be no. I did not."

"Whatever." Robin waved away the explanation. "It must have worked."

Shaking my head did little to clear the mist created by trying to follow her train of thought. "Anyway." What had I come there to ask again? Oh, right. "There's a rumor going around that Jober Peavey was causing you some trouble."

Whoops. Touched a nerve there.

Robin's face went red, sparks flared behind her eyes. "That jerk owes me a pink car."

A dull throb settled into my temples. "Excuse me."

"Gesundheit."

The throb ramped up from easy listening to a rock beat. "I don't...I didn't...never mind. Tell me about the pink car."

Instead, Robin reached over and brushed the hair back from my face. "You should be using brown mascara instead of black. It would go much better with your coloring. And maybe a dark, berry lip stain. I could give you a makeover and a discount if you wanted to host a party."

"No, I don't think so." But the dominoes had begun to fall. "You're a beauty consultant? And you were trying to win a car, but Jober—"

"Convinced half the women in town that I was in a cult and the makeover parties were how we recruit new members. I lost several bookings."

Boom. There it was.

"How many parties have you done?" If she'd been close to winning a car, she might have had a motive for murder.

"Oh, just a couple, and one was practice."

"And how many does it take to win a car?"

Sensing false interest, Robin warmed up. "A lot, and I'd need to recruit eleven more consultants for my sales team. It takes twelve, but my cousin just signed up, so that's one down. Were you interested?"

I held up a hand to stave off that line of questioning. "No, but thanks anyway. Did you have words with Jober over his allegations?"

"We don't have those in Maine. I think they only live in the south. But anyway, I did say something to Jober." Robin stopped near her car, cocked a hip, and snapped her fingers back and forth three times. "Gave him a piece of my mind right there in the grocery store."

Did it come with a magnifying glass? I wondered.

"Lucky I did, too. Lorna Post was in line behind him, and when she heard what I had to say, she booked a party for next week, so I'm back in business. She's got a big mouth, so if she likes her makeover, I figure I'll get a few new bookings."

We'd arrived at Robin's car by then, and while I tried to think of a way to maneuver the conversation around to her whereabouts at the time of the murder, she opened the door. "I've got samples of that lip stain if you want one." But instead of reaching for one, she flipped down her visor and pulled a piece of used chewing gum from the back side of it.

When she popped the dust-coated wad in her mouth, I lost the will to live. And nearly lost my lunch as well.

"Thanks, I'm all set." The time for subtle had passed. "Did you kill Jober Peavey?"

Robin wrinkled her nose. "Ew. No. What a horrible

thing to ask." She shuddered. "Besides, plenty of people had more of a reason than me to want him gone."

It almost hurt me to ask, but I had to. "Who?"

"Huh?" Robin gave me a blank look.

"Who might have wanted to murder Jober Peavey? Besides you, I mean."

"Didn't I just say I didn't want to kill him?" The nasty gum snapped and popped. I couldn't stop watching her mouth. "You should probably talk to Adam."

"The cook at Cappy's?"

Robin nodded. "Yeah. He's killed once already, so why not do it again?"

CHAPTER SIXTEEN

atching Robin drive away, I pulled my phone out of my pocket and speed-dialed Jacy's number.

"Adam, the cook at Cappy's" I said when she answered.

"What about him?"

"I just talked to Robin," I said.

"Nothing good can come of that."

Even though she couldn't see me, I raised my hand. "Testify. But she did tell me I should wear brown mascara instead of black. And—" I paused for dramatic effect. "She said we should talk to Adam because he'd already killed once."

There was silence on the other end of the line.

"Jace, you still there?"

"I'm here. Just trying to process."

Since most conversations with or about Robin ended that way, I gave her a few seconds, then pressed. "You know him better than I do since the extent of my entire experience with the man is food-related and from a distance. What do you think? Is it possible?"

"I'd give it a 1.3 on the scale of maybe. Who was he supposed to have killed?"

Having walked back to my car, I got in, started the engine, and cranked up the heat. "No idea. I was too dumbfounded to ask."

I could almost hear Jacy nodding. "Robin does seem to have that effect on people. Anyway, here's the sum of my knowledge of Adam. He moved here from Iowa, or maybe Ohio. Utah? I can't remember exactly, but it's one of the four-letter states."

"When?"

Another pause while she thought. I cranked the blower up to five and warmed my fingers while I waited.

"Around the same time as Jober, now that you mention it. Coincidental, no?"

Even though she couldn't see me, I shrugged. "Maybe, but it doesn't seem likely since Jober wasn't from any of the four-letter states. Still, if there's a scandal in Adam's past and Jober found out about it, that could go to motive."

Then again, if shutting Jober up was the motive for his murder, the suspect list grew longer by the day. And why weren't my fingers getting any warmer?

The answer to that question came when Davina popped into view. "I've got to go, Jace." I hung up and turned to face my spectral passenger. "What can I do for you, Davina?"

"How do you do it?"

"Do what? The hokey-pokey? It's easy...you put your left foot in."

I paid for the sarcasm with most of my body heat as ice crystals made patterns on the inside of my windows.

"Very funny."

"You'll need to be more specific if you want an answer."

"Technically, your left foot has nothing to do with the hokey-pokey, which is a separate action performed after the appendage has been both put in and taken out."

Spinning in my seat, I stared at her. "What's your boggle, Davina? I'm sure you didn't pop in here to discuss the finer points of silly dance songs."

"I prefer Scrabble to Boggle, but anyway. This Jober character is driving me nuts. He keeps popping up wherever I go, and I thought if I talked to him, I could get him to see that you're only trying to help him. Then, maybe, he'd talk to you."

"I take it things didn't go to plan?"

"Not hardly, and he is the most annoying person I've ever met."

A bit more of the windshield cleared. "That seems to be the popular opinion. What's he doing besides following you around?"

Davina lifted a hand to rub her forehead. Did ghosts get headaches?

"Spouting fire and brimstone, for one thing. Doesn't

matter. I'll handle him, but you should know he's giving off a vibe, which worries me."

Great. "What kind of vibe?"

Pausing for a moment, Davina framed her answer simply. "Guilt. It simply rolls off him if you know what to look for, and in my former line of work, I saw plenty of it, so I do. I mean, I'm not an expert or anything, but I know what I know, and I see what I see. It's blocking him, and I'm worried."

I held up both hands. "I'm not arguing the point because you're making perfect sense. He saw deceit and treachery in almost everyone he met. That skewed point of view had to be coming from something that lived inside him, and guilt seems about right to me."

"You care, don't you?" Davina sized me up. "Not necessarily about Jober Peavey himself, but you want to help him find peace, and not just because that's the only way to get him out of your life."

"Wouldn't you?"

Nodding, Davina faded, leaving me to drive home with only my thoughts for companions.

Given the hectic nature of the recent past, I was in the mood for comfort food, fuzzy socks, and cuddling in front of a good movie with my dog at my feet. To get a start on the comfort food, I smothered half a chicken in a simple marinade made with onions, garlic, fresh thyme, and plenty of olive oil. Tender and flavorful, the chicken would go perfectly with a pan of roasted winter vegetables—

carrots, parsnips, onions, sweet potatoes, and a bulb of fennel.

My wrist ached a bit, but I managed to peel and chop everything, added olive oil and chives, then a couple of grinds of pepper and some pink sea salt. The sweet and licorice scents of fennel and parsnips clung to my fingers even after a good wash, lifting my mood.

When Drew walked in after his last class of the day, he stopped just inside the door, sniffed the air, and sighed. "I think I just stumbled into heaven."

"Points for the appreciation." I grinned and went into his arms for a welcome home kiss.

"And there's my own personal angel," he said after letting me go.

"Minor deduction for the cheese factor," I grinned at him. "Another kiss should wipe your slate, though."

He didn't hesitate to oblige, and all talk of ghosts and death was off the table for the rest of the evening.

Refreshed after an evening of what constitutes normalcy in my life, I walked into my bank the next morning expecting to speak to Mr. Herbert, who had worked there for as long as I could remember. As a friend of my dad's. Mr. Herbert was someone I trusted. But once I explained the reason for my visit, the teller shook her head.

"Mr. Herbert retired recently," she said. "But our new manager is available, and he'd be the best person to help you. His office is just there, and since he's not with anyone at the moment, you can go right in."

"Thanks." As it did whenever I took a moment to think about the ridiculous sum of money Kitty had practically forced on me, butterflies with razor wings took flight in my stomach. But Patrea had been right, I would feel better if I took the reins of the trust into my own hands, and I needed a banker's advice.

After a deep breath, I stepped through the open door.

"Excuse me. My name is Everly Dupree. The teller told me it was okay to just come in."

Apparently, I carry some sort of bank manager bias

when it comes to age because the man who rose and reached across the desk to offer a firm handshake was younger than I expected. Not too bad on the eyes, either, for someone who had at least fifteen years on me.

"Martin Walker, what can I do for you?" A touch of gray painted wings against the nut-brown at his temples. He looked vaguely familiar, but I couldn't place where I'd seen him before. Probably at one or another of the town functions.

"As I said, I'm Everly Dupree, and I've recently come into some money. A lot of money, actually. Not, I suppose, that it will seem like a lot to you since you deal with large sums of money every day, but to me, it's an overwhelming amount." I'd begun to babble, which doesn't happen often, but I find it hard to stop when it does.

Mr. Walker smiled, leaned back in his chair, and tilted his head. "Sounds like you've come to the right place, then." He offered a charming smile intended to put me at ease. "What do you need?"

The smile went some way toward settling me down. A stern, inner talking-to finished the task and straightened my spine. "The money was put in a trust with me being both sole recipient and trustee, so I thought it would be a good idea to transfer the entire balance to my account here."

As I talked, I pulled the trust paperwork from my over-sized bag and showed him the amount in question and the terms of the trust. Slate-gray eyes widened as his gaze flicked to my face, then back down, and his posture changed subtly.

"Under the terms listed, I see no reason why we can't help you make the transfer. It will take several days, you understand." A wider smile accompanied the warning.

I nodded that I did. Paul may have been the one in our relationship with control of all the money, but I wasn't a total rube, either. It just felt different being the one with the stuffed checkbook for once.

"I'm in no great hurry." The last of my nerves went blissfully quiet.

"You'll need a financial advisor. Someone you can trust. It's not necessarily in my job description these days, but I'd be happy to personally fill that role for you. This is a lot of money, and you'd do better if you had someone whose job it is to look out for your best interests."

Taking a moment to put the trust paperwork away, I let him down as easily as possible. "I appreciate the offer, but I'm working with someone in that capacity already. I mainly came in to talk to Mr. Herbert about the mechanics of getting the money here. He's always been so helpful, but I didn't know he planned to retire."

"These things happen." Walker shrugged, and, his tone still genial, he suggested I open a second account for the money from the trust. "Then, it's as simple as writing a personal check for the full amount. You'll need to contact the originating bank to close the account, but that shouldn't be a problem." Finished, he shook my hand again and gave me what sounded like a canned speech about being happy to help me with all my banking needs.

"Please consider my offer, and if you change your mind about needing help with financial planning, let me know."

I thanked him again and headed out to do the rest of my errands, feeling good about having taken a step forward.

CHAPTER EIGHTEEN

Next on my list for the day, I drove to Pine Tree Automotive to get my car serviced and grill a potential suspect.

"You sure she's not for sale?" As he always did, Bennie caressed the hood of my car, his eyes gleaming with the admiration certain men only save for hunks of metal and tires. "I'd give you top dollar."

"Not today." I smiled and dashed his hopes yet again. "I've got other plans for her." Which was true even if I meant to have something better for winter driving before the first flakes took to the air this year. Since those plans meant keeping the Buick in the family, I gently turned him down.

"She's one fine machine." He sat in the seat for a moment and rested his hands on the wheel before releasing the hood latch. "They don't make them like this anymore."

"My dad says the same thing." Which was why he'd appreciate the car far more than I did. Not that I was complaining because I wasn't, but it felt like the right time to move on.

It was also time to get to the second reason for my visit. I opened with something noncommittal and watched his face. "Shame about Mr. Peavey."

Bennie lost his ever-cheerful smile as he used a funny-looking tool to loosen the oil filter. "A worse shame if they pin his murder on Milo. No way that guy would shove a knife in someone's back. He's too damn nice."

Being nice wasn't a guarantee against being a murderer, but I agreed with his assessment, so I nodded and let my silence goad him into saying more. "And he definitely wouldn't go after Oddjob since Milo was the only person in town who liked the man. Jober wasn't the easiest guy to be around."

Sounded like he spoke from experience.

"Yes, I figured that out at Cappy's on Friday when he threatened half the bar with airing their dirty laundry. I figure someone's was filthier than the rest, and they really didn't want it hung on the line for public viewing."

Bennie shrugged the suggestion off and, while the old oil drained, used another weird tool to squirt some fairly stinky grease into a series of fittings.

"Mooselick River is a small town. Close-knit, like family." He pulled a red rag out of his back pocket and wiped off excess grease. "Which means secrets have a way of eventually coming out. People like to talk, and if they can't find anything interesting to say, they'll make something up."

"Do you think Oddjob was making things up? He

certainly talked like he had dirt on a lot of people." What the heck, I figured, go bold or go home. "And when he started singling people out, I thought you were one of them. Or maybe the guy sitting next to you."

I watched him closely for signs of prevarication, but his gaze met mine steadily. He was either an exceptional bluffer, which I doubted because I'd heard about his lack of prowess at poker, or he had nothing to hide.

Bennie frowned. "You mean the new guy from the bank?"

"Martin Walker?" No wonder he'd looked familiar.

"That's the guy." The mechanic grinned ruefully, and held up a hand, then pointed to himself. "I don't know about him, but I'm the one Jober called a cheat."

"Do tell."

"Oddjob was convinced I'd cheated him out of twenty dollars when he brought his truck in for brake pads. It looked like a simple job, but the stupid thing had a sticky caliper, and I had to put in a new set of slides. They cost extra, and even though I gave him the parts at cost, he didn't think he should have to pay."

He popped the new oil filter on, double-checked to make sure it was tight, then hit the release on the lift to lower Sally back down on four wheels.

"Recently?"

Bennie shook his head. "No." He paused a moment to think. "It was a few years back. Not long after he moved to town, but he refused to let it go. I offered to give him the twenty bucks back just to shut him up, but that made things worse because he took it as an admission of guilt instead of good customer service."

He held his left fist up. "Rock." Then the other. "Hard place." Then he leaned forward to put his head between them. "And there was me in the space between. I can't have been the only one he treated that way. There was no pleasing him."

"A glass-half-empty kind of guy."

After a moment's search to find a cleaner one, Bennie wiped his hands on a rag. "I guess. Except he'd point out that his glass was half empty, then accuse you of drinking his drink. Between you and me, someone who's that suspicious of everyone else's motives is someone who has something to hide."

Not the first time I'd heard that theory. Probably wouldn't be the last, either.

"So you weren't surprised to hear he'd been killed?"

"I suppose I should say yes, and how he was a saint because that's what some folks do when a person's dead, but I wasn't surprised. Jober was a jerk, and if he decided not to like someone, he'd believe the worst of them no matter what. Not too hard to figure someone got tired of their good name being dragged through the mud."

Nothing ominous in what he said, nor were there any revelations.

"Like he did yours?"

"Meh," Bennie said. "People have said way worse

things about me, and most of that stuff was true. Jober didn't bother me none."

So much for Bennie as a suspect, and I was okay with that since I hadn't wanted to be wrong about him.

"Vernon French had more reason to want Jober gone than I ever did. Pretty sure he wasn't the only one. Not by a long stretch."

The name sounded familiar, but I couldn't think why, so I shook my head.

"He's the road commissioner," Bennie filled in the gap in my knowledge. "Grew up right here in town. His mother is a cousin to Brian Dean's mother."

I followed the twists of that family tree until a bell rang in my head. "Oh! You mean Dibble?"

A shrug was my answer. "I only know him as Vernon. Or Vern, I guess."

"Dibble is a childhood nickname." One I probably shouldn't bandy about since it had its roots in the word dribble, and that's something a grown man probably doesn't do anymore. "I can't believe I've been back for over a year and didn't know he was the road commissioner."

The simple answer to that was outside of helping Martha put on a series of town functions and the occasional Friday night out with the girls, I hadn't socialized a lot since my return to town. An oversight I intended to maintain.

"It's recent. He only took on the job in March when his

father decided to retire and pass the equipment on to him, and he was at Cappy's that night. Him and his wife. Sitting about three barstools down from where I was."

Close enough to have been in Jober's line of sight when he went off on his diatribe.

"Hell of a nice guy, you ask me, and a good head for business, too. Takes the blame for every pothole that pops up around here but does his best to keep the roads passable on what the town agrees to pay, which ain't nearly enough. I mean, he does okay with his day job, but it don't seem fair to expect him to be out all hours of the night plowing for next to no money."

By then, I'd followed Bennie into his office to pay my bill. While I ran my card through the reader, I asked the obvious question. "Any idea what beef Jober might have had with Dibble, I mean Vernon?"

The card reader beeped to signal the end of my transaction, and Bennie shrugged. "Listen, you ask anyone who ever had to deal with Jober, and you'll hear the same story. He'd listen to about half of what was said, then cook up some damn fool story no one in their right mind would believe."

That meshed with what I'd learned about the man so far.

"Except Jober did. Or that's how it seemed to me. He'd lost the line between truth and imagination. The chin-wagging was mostly harmless, but Jober cost Vern a big paving contract this time."

"How big of a contract?" I wondered out loud. "Worth killing over?"

"Big. I figure it came out to a solid six figures worth of income. Listen, I know that's a lot of money, but this happened in May, so it's been several months. I guess you can do your own math on that, but mine doesn't come out to Vern being a killer."

"Revenge is a dish best served cold," I said. "I have no idea who coined the phrase, but it could apply here."

Grinning, Bennie shrugged. "You got a guy who digs holes for a living. He wants to kill someone, I'm thinking that person ends up six feet under in a secluded spot where no one will ever look."

"Okay, that's a valid point, but even so, people sometimes do things in the heat of the moment."

Frustration fired Bennie up. "It's either cold revenge or heat of the moment. It can't be both. You're talking smack about a guy who dips into his own pockets to pay for extra help when the town funding runs short, which it does on a regular basis."

Holding up a finger to indicate I should wait, he selected a sticker and wrote the date and mileage on it with sharp motions, slapped it on the windshield, then turned.

"I know you're in deep with Martha Tipton and her intentions are good with all these events to raise funds for a new playground and whatnot, but some of the money should go back into our infrastructure. It will take more to make this town thrive again than a few new swings and some fancy signs."

His opinion carried some heat. Enough to make me look at him differently.

"You should run for town office this spring. I'd vote for you."

I could see the thought pleased him, but he demurred all the same. "Who'd take me seriously? Half the older generation still thinks of me as Bad Boy Bennie. Once people get an idea in their head, it's nearly impossible to get it back out. You do things when you're young and stupid, and I'll own up because I'd be an idiot to try and deny what everyone knows, but I'm not that guy anymore."

Because he seemed to need the reassurance, I patted the mechanic on the arm and said, "If it's any consolation, my dad recommends you highly to anyone who asks where to take their car for repairs."

"Thanks. Your dad's a good man."

"I agree." To relieve the tension between us, I changed the subject and asked for a recommendation on whether four-wheel drive or all-wheel drive made for better handling on winter roads.

The answer came with far more technical detail than I really needed, but in the end, I had a list of things to look for, the names of reputable dealerships, and an offer that if I went for a used car, he'd take a look at it to make sure I didn't get screwed.

"*You're* a good man, Bennie. And I don't just mean for offering to watch out for my wallet. Let me know if you ever change your mind about becoming a force in town business. You'll have my support a hundred percent."

I left the garage minus one suspect but with a line on two more. All in all, I supposed that counted as progress.

CHAPTER NINETEEN

"It's not breaking and entering if you have a key." Who was I trying to convince?

"It is if you're doing it in the dead of night." Jacy wasn't buying it. "Which we are, and you don't have the key yet."

I huffed out a breath and risked aiming the dim light of my phone screen into the open mouth of the dog-shaped bird feeder where Davina had hidden her extra key. Call me a weenie, but there could have been spiders or something worse in there.

"I do, now." Seeing nothing creepy or crawly, I stuck my hand in and closed my fingers over cool metal. The little box with a key embossed on the lid got caught behind the dog's teeth. I had to give it a yank to pull it free. "And you can just climb right down off that high horse of yours before it tosses you over the fence. We wouldn't even be here if your mother hadn't told you where the hide-a-key was and offered to keep Davina busy while we searched for something to help find her killer."

Which was the point of this whole operation.

"It's fun, though, right?" Irrepressible, Jacy let go of her mock annoyance and did a little dance. "I feel like a kid sneaking out after curfew, hoping not to get caught."

The lid refused to come off the key box, so I applied more force, grunting with the effort. "Stupid thing must be rusted shut. Here," I handed Jacy my phone, "hold this up so I can see what's going on."

She did, and in the weak light, I saw the shine of a piece of tape. "No wonder it won't open. It's taped over."

"Give it." Jacy handed me back my phone and snatched the box away from me. "I've got nails of steel." She used a fingernail to pierce the tape, then snapped the lid open and pulled out the key.

I grabbed her hand and looked at her nails. "Black polish?"

"Excuse me if I dressed for the job at hand. You sure you want to go through with this?"

"What choice do I have. Davina's been holding out on me, and I need a solid lead if I don't want her to become a permanent fixture in my life. She has to cross over soon." For more reasons than that she was a less than genial house guest at times. "She's driving your mother nuts, too."

Dressed in black from head to toe, Jacy opened the back door and slipped inside. "Why do you think I agreed to this little mission in the first place? Momma Wade's wildest dream came true. She can see a ghost, but the experience isn't living up to the hype, so she's in a state. I can't have her in a state because she refuses to live there alone, and I'm tired of the daily commute. I'm all in with whatever needs to happen to get this mess over and let all our lives return to normal."

Closing the door behind me, I said, "I'm not sure I'd recognize normal if it walked up and slapped me in the face, but by all means, let's get this done."

When Jacy stopped short, I nearly plowed into her.

"Wait," she said. "Are you sure Davina doesn't know we're here?"

"I didn't take out an ad in the Ghostly Times if that's what you're asking. But we should be fine so long as Leandra does her part." I brushed past her and made my way deeper into the house. "I can't tell if Davina's holding out on me because she's got something to hide or if she sincerely believes no one in her personal sphere would resort to murder."

Using one hand as a shield, Jacy shined her keychain penlight around to get her bearings. "Well, someone did, and I think my mother is still on Ernie's radar. He acted like she was lying when she said she didn't know Davina planned to leave the shop to her."

"She's not the only one. I don't think Ernie's still looking hard at her, but my mother is still under orders not to leave town. Maybe we'll find something to get them both off the hook."

A typical example of New England architecture, I expected to find a warren of rooms inside the two-story house, but someone—possibly Davina—had given the place an interior facelift. Being a homeowner myself, I'd developed an interest in home remodeling, so allowed myself to get distracted.

"You can tell this used to be two rooms." Even with all the blinds closed, I wouldn't chance more light than what came off the screen of my cell phone, and that wasn't enough to illuminate the spacious living room. "If you look at the ceiling, you can kind of see the patched area where the wall used to be. It really opened up the space a lot."

"Mmhmm," was Jacy's response.

"Makes me think seriously about taking down the wall between that front parlor and the sitting room at my place."

"A little less DIY and a little more B&E, please," Jacy sounded impatient. "I'd rather not have to call my husband for bail money because we fooled around too long and got busted."

"You're right," I conceded but took a mental snapshot anyway. "I'll take the upstairs." So what if I wanted to see what she'd done up there, too. I'd been in my place long enough the feeling of being a guest in someone else's home had begun to dissipate. It was time to think about making some changes. "You look around down here."

The stairs terminated in a hallway shaped like an upside-down and backward L with a protective railing running along the long side. At the top of the stairs, I peered into the bedroom on the right, which was nicely decorated, but clearly not used for anything other than a spare. Two more rooms lined the longer leg of the L, the smallest a bathroom that had been gutted for remodeling, the other pressed into storage for the materials waiting to be installed.

At that point, I almost wished I hadn't come. Seeing the stacked tile and bathroom fixtures picked out by a woman who would never see the finished product brought a sting of pity. There was nothing here that would help me find Davina's killer.

At the end of the hall, the last door opened into a closet crammed with plastic garment bags that gave off enough static to make my hair float. But the thick script in black marker on the flap of a cardboard box on top a bin of Christmas decorations really gave me the tinglies.

Fan Mail. Jackpot.

"I found something," I called down to Jacy.

"So did I," she said from the bottom of the stairs. "Check this out." She came up to join me.

Windowless, the closet wouldn't give us away, so I closed the door behind us and yanked the string pull on the bare bulb light fixture. Jacy blinked in the sudden brightness of what had to be a 100-watt bulb.

"Fifty bucks says mine's better than yours." Grinning, Jacy plopped a portable fire safe on top of the stack of fan mail boxes. "I found this under the bed." She flipped the latches. "It's not even locked."

The lid was heavier than it looked and thicker, too, but there was enough space inside for a sheaf of Davina's most important documents. I lifted out and set aside a copy of her will, the deed to the house, her birth certificate, and the title to her car.

"Or not." Disgusted by the ordinariness of the contents, Jacy slapped a hand on my shoulder. "I guess it's a good thing you didn't take that bet."

Except my case of the tinglies had turned into a full-on bout of the shivers. "Don't count yourself out just yet." At the very bottom of the safe lay an envelope with the address of a courthouse in New Jersey. "This could be something."

When I unfolded the sheets, and we got a look at the heading, Jacy and I exchanged a look, and then I cursed Davina's name six ways to Sunday. She'd been holding back, and it would serve her right if I left her ghostly backside swinging in the ether for all eternity.

"Davina had a baby," Jacy whispered.

"And gave it up for adoption." My tone was dark with both pity and frustration. "Clearly, she didn't think that was information I needed to know."

I waved the papers under Jacy's nose, then quirked an eyebrow when she snatched them from me, laid them out one by one, and snapped her fingers at me.

"What?" I said.

"Give me your phone." When I did, she clicked off several photos of each page, put them back in the envelope, and replaced everything else the way it had been. "I'll put this back where I found it while you get that box of fan mail open. I feel creepy even being in here all of a sudden."

Jacy wasn't the only one.

Since I didn't have her nails of steel, I tried using the edge of Davina's key to cut the tape. Ernie should have already been there and done that, and I'd have thought he would have found the fire safe by now as well. But then again, he'd had the missing persons case tangled in with the murder on top of busting up a drug ring. He'd probably been more concerned with finding clues at the actual crime scene, and as soon as he'd made an arrest, another murder dropped in his lap. It made sense for something to fall through the cracks.

For that reason, I debated just taking the whole box of fan mail home with me. Combing through the letters for clues would take time I didn't have right now. The longer we hung around, the higher our chances of getting busted. Having Ernie show up here would be just one circle of hell below having Davina catch me going through her things.

The hell with that. I dragged the box to the floor with my good hand, kicked it toward the top of the stairs, and met Jacy coming back up.

"I'm bringing this home."

Nodding, Jacy grabbed the box for me, turned, and

preceded me back down. "Wouldn't that be construed as evidence tampering?" She didn't say I shouldn't, though.

"Probably. But I don't care. Ernie has so much on his plate that he probably won't push on Davina's case right away. It's up to us to find something."

"Then let's do this. We'll be partners in crime."

If this came back to bite us, I'd cover her butt and let Ernie use mine as a chew toy.

"Better if we're partners in crime solving," I said.

Stopping short so I almost ran into her, Jacy turned. "Whatever it is, I'm here for it."

We left the house the way we'd come in, but I put the key in my pocket for when it was time to return the box of fan mail.

CHAPTER TWENTY

"You look like a truck guy, and it's your lucky day because we've got some great deals on pickups right now." A gleam in his eye, the salesman at the car dealership practically pounced on Drew the minute we walked through the door. For all the attention he gave me, I might as well have been a fly on Drew's arm.

"Thanks, but I'm looking for something in a crossover. All wheel drive," I spoke up, but the guy's attention remained riveted to Drew as if I wasn't even there.

Drew, bless him, merely lifted a brow and pointedly turned his head in my direction, thinking, I assume, that the salesman would do the same.

Nope.

"Every one of our trucks qualifies for a special interest loan, but you'd have to act fast because this deal ends tomorrow."

I fished around in my purse for the wrinkled notepad sheet with Bennie's logo on it and read off the name of the woman he recommended I talk to.

"Is Clarice Dunn available?" I asked, but the guy kept talking to Drew, who was visibly annoyed at this point.

"Look. I get that you're trying to make a sale here, but I'm not in the market for a truck."

Drew tried. I'll give him that, and I'm not sure if anyone was more surprised than him when I hit my limit. "Clarice Dunn, are you here?" I practically yelled.

"What do you want with her?" His face reddening, the guy had never even bothered to give us his name, and whatever happened to wearing name tags? "She doesn't know anything about trucks."

"No one is buying a truck today," I said as a woman poked her head out the door of one of the offices to our left. "Clarice Dunn?" I turned my attention to her, and when she nodded, walked away to leave Drew to brush off Mr. Brush Cut.

"My friend Bennie spoke very highly of you. I'm looking for a crossover SUV with all-wheel drive." I smiled hopefully. "Not a truck, okay? Not even if they're on sale or whatever."

Clarice smiled back and adhered to proper workplace etiquette by not making a derogatory remark about her co-worker, but she did wink at me. "No problem. Any friend of Bennie's gets the VIP treatment from me. Let's go see what we have on the lot."

On our way past, I tucked my arm around Drew's and pulled gently to extricate him from the clutches of the truck-obsessed salesman, who still hadn't stopped talking. "Excuse me, but he's not buying a truck today, okay?"

"The little lady put her foot down, eh?"

Drew met the salesman's sneer with a level look. "If you'd bothered to listen, I was never in the market for a truck, and even if I was, I don't do business with idiots."

We'd never know what might have happened next because my bank manager, Martin Walker, walked through the door and, when he saw me, came over to shake my hand.

"Ms. Dupree. Nice to see you again." Then, to my utter embarrassment, he turned to the truck pusher and said, "Take good care of this one. She'll probably pay cash because she's got plenty to burn."

"If you'll excuse us." I threw Clarice Dunn a save-me look, and she didn't disappoint. Nor was she able to hide a triumphant smile. But I wouldn't hold that against her.

"Thanks," I said when we were finally outside. "I was beginning to choke on all the testosterone in the air." Drew's arm got a pat. He was definitely one of the good ones.

In the end, I did pay cash, and I bought exactly what I wanted, a car very similar to the one I'd left behind in my divorce, only this time in bright, screaming red. I had to wait a week to take delivery, but it was a small price to pay to get what I wanted. My ex-husband would have called the color ostentatious, but screw him. This was for me.

CHAPTER TWENTY-ONE

When Patrea strolled through the inn's front door long before the end of her normal business hours, her expression cheerful only on the surface, I could tell something was wrong.

"What's up?" With leaf-peeping season over and Thanksgiving weeks away, the inn was quiet, so I'd been catching up on my reading while I filled in for David. When she approached, I motioned for her to join me behind the desk and used my foot to drag out the extra bar stool we used when there were two of us back there on busy days.

Patrea hoisted herself on the stool, rested her elbows on the desk before answering. "Not my business, that's for sure. I've had several clients call this week offering a variety of reasons for why they no longer require my help with their legal matters." She made air quotes.

Reaching out, I gave her a quick, one-armed hug. "I'm sorry. If it's any consolation, I fully believe this will pass once Davina's murder is solved. It's just that in these small towns, people are quick to get keyed up and blow things all out of proportion, but they're also quick to forget."

She shrugged. "That's not even the problem."

"Can I help?"

"You can tell me if I've lost my mind because I'm not even that upset about losing clients. I probably should be, but I did a lot of thinking during my enforced vacation in the big house."

I let my tone go dry. "Big house might be a bit of an exaggeration."

That got a chuckle out of her.

"Point taken." She circled a finger to indicate the entire inn. "The truth is, I'd rather be doing this."

"Running the inn? I don't think David's looking for help right now. Or were you thinking of making an offer on it?"

I'd apparently missed the point because she shook her head and grinned.

"He couldn't afford me in any case, but what I meant was the restoration process. I'm not saying the legal needs in this town are boring, but they totally are. A good para-legal could handle most of the day-to-day work and free me up to pursue a passion project. I think I want to try my hand at flipping a house."

Sometimes the universe conspires to drop the perfect opportunity right in your lap. This was one of those times.

"I actually know someone. One of Leo's tenants is finishing up a course in paralegal training, and since her mother just moved in with her to help keep an eye on her son, she was hoping to ask you for a full-time job. Then you got arrested, and she figured she'd lost her chance. I'd be happy to give you Jane's number."

Considering this, Patrea tilted her head to give the matter some thought. "What's she like?"

"I haven't spent a ton of time with her, but she seems nice enough. She's never late with her rent, so I'd say dependable. Maybe not a ball of fire in the personality department, but I suspect that's down to being the single parent of a high-energy son. Little Jamie's a handful."

Light dawned. "Toy soldiers in the sink?"

"The very same."

"I've seen her around. She always looks dazed."

I leaned over and lowered my voice even though there wasn't anyone around to hear. "Between you and me, her son is adorable, but I seriously doubt she's had a good night's sleep since he was born."

Today was about to become Patrea's day because Leo decided he wasn't interested in Jane's mother's Victorian fixer-upper.

"What's more, Jane's mother has a gingerbread Victorian she's looking to sell. It needs some TLC, so that might be a good flip project. I showed it to Leo on my way over here, but he wasn't interested."

"What are you? My fairy godmother?"

Laughing, I mimicked waving a wand, then said, "You might not think so when you see the place. Leo had first dibs and passed because it was more than he wanted to take on."

The comment did nothing to deter her. If anything, Patrea's eyes gleamed brighter at the possible enormity of the challenge.

"To be fair," I said, "the house is too big to make a good rental, but it's not quite big enough to convert into a duplex. And I did try to discourage Leo from doing that because it would have ruined all the house's charm."

"But it has charm, right?"

I nodded. "I think it's a perfect fit for what you want to do. The house is a bit older than mine, but the interior has a similar feel. Lots of vintage wallpaper, the floors need refinishing, and there's some truly tragic linoleum in the kitchen. Vintage seventies is my guess."

"You had me at gingerbread. I have to see it. Do you still have the keys?"

Pulling the angel keyring out of my pocket, I dangled it in front of her. "I do. I'll need to call Jane and let her know I'm taking you through, and you'll have to wait," I checked the clock on the wall, "another ten minutes until Nanette's shift starts."

"You go ahead now." Half a second before her voice lifted me half out of my skin, I smelled the floral scent of cleaning solution that followed Nanette like a cloud.

"What are you wearing? Some kind of sneaky ninja shoes or something?"

Nanette grinned. "Crepe soles. Easier on the feet when

you're on them all day, and quiet, too. Gives me a chance to eavesdrop on people." Completely unapologetic, she said, "That house sounds perfect, and I'm here, so you can go ahead and look at it."

For some reason, the dismissal struck me wrong. Maybe it was her tone, or maybe it was the speculative way she looked at Patrea.

"I told David I'd stay the full shift."

"Suit yourself, but that one's just about bouncing in her chair." Nanette came around to the front of the desk. She nodded toward Patrea. "I never pegged you for a killer, by the way. You're definitely not the type. Too upright."

"Thanks, I guess."

"I also think Ernie could have waited until you were in a more private setting to make the arrest. You ask me, that was some serious showboating."

Patrea and I exchanged a look. "I didn't know you were at Cappy's last Friday. Where were you sitting?" And more importantly, do I need to add you to our list of suspects?

"Front table near the bandstand. Close enough to ogle the lead singer, but not close enough to get a good look at the guy having the tantrum. Who knew he'd end up dead?"

Mentally assessing her location, I realized she couldn't possibly have been in Jober's line of sight when he went off on his tirade, so she wouldn't be added to our list. I might have pursued the matter further, but Patrea shot me a desperate glance, accompanied by a subtle nod toward the door.

Rising, I gave in. "I guess I can let you take over a few minutes early." When Patrea nearly tipped over her chair in her haste to stand, Nanette let out a low chuckle and waved toward the door.

"Go."

We did.

Outside, I pulled out my phone, called Jane, and quickly got permission to take Patrea through the house.

"If this is half as good as I'm hoping, I'll owe you baked goods for a year," Patrea promised.

"I'm partial to chocolate croissants, in case you're wondering."

"Duly noted. I'll drive," she said. The implication being we'd get there sooner.

"No need," I led the way past the parking lot and crunched through browned grass on the frost-dead lawn. "It's back here." The gabled peak just showed over the tops of the trees bordering the far end of the property.

Patrea stopped dead in her tracks. "You said gingerbread Victorian. You didn't say it was *that* gingerbread Victorian. But it's not listed for sale. There's no sign, and I detour past that place every other day just to check."

"It's not listed, but if you don't snatch it up, it will be."

Walking quickly now to keep up with Patrea's long-legged stride, I nearly tumbled down the stone steps leading from the inn's lawn to the street that ran along behind it. Nothing like following after a woman on a mission.

"Hurry up. I'm dying here."

"Good thing there wasn't any traffic. You didn't even look both ways." I caught up with her on the front porch, but she waved a dismissive hand. "Don't you even want to hear the price before you go inside?"

"Nope." Head shake for emphasis. "I don't even care. This house was meant for me. I knew that the first time I clapped eyes on it. They don't make corbels like this anymore. Where's the key?"

I pulled the ring out again and didn't resist when she snatched it out of my hand. Watching the reserved attorney get all gooey over carved wood was more fun than I thought it would be.

"Just remember," I said. "Jane's mom could change her mind, and all of her things are still here. She'll need some time to pare down."

Already disappearing into the darkened interior, all I saw of Patrea was her hand waving over her shoulder. "She can take all the time she needs so long as we have a contract in place for the purchase. I won't be able to start on the exterior until spring anyway."

"Okay." I followed her inside, where she'd already begun recording voice notes into her phone for the work she intended to do.

"It has parquet floors." Dropping to her knees, Patrea

ignored any dust that might collect on her stylish trousers in pale gray and ran her hand along the bordered edge of the floor. "Little loose in spots. Definitely needs refinishing, but this isn't bad at all."

Standing, she brushed some dust from her knees and moved deeper into the house, muttering plans in some sort of verbal shorthand that I didn't fully understand. I caught up with her in a kitchen that looked a bit like mine with lace curtains and older appliances.

"Kitchen's a reno rather than a resto. Needs an update with all the mod-cons."

Cocking an eyebrow, I fixed her with a look. "A what with the what?"

"Renovation rather than restoration. I can keep the molding and see if I can get them to sell me that gorgeous enameled Hoosier to maintain something of the period feel, but kitchens sell houses. This one needs an update to bring in the modern conveniences."

Crossing the room, she poked at a spot on the wall that bulged slightly.

"See that?" Prodding caused the bulge to give a little. "The plaster's lost its keys."

I shook my head and frowned. "Keys?"

"This is a lath and plaster wall. The laths would be nailed horizontally to the studs leaving space enough for plaster to be pushed in between and form keys that hold the plaster to the laths. When the keys fail, you get this sort of bubble effect behind sections that have come loose."

"I see." It made perfect sense when she explained it that way. "So you'll need to knock out the loose bits and patch in new?"

She shrugged. "I could, but instead, I'll take it down to the studs, add insulation to make the place easier to heat, and have fresh, smooth walls. A house like this? It's about finding the balance between period and modern while meeting new building codes."

"The way Jane talked," I said, "I expected to find the house in far worse shape than it looks."

After a moment's consideration, Patrea pointed out some mismatched trim in the downstairs hallway. "This was a recent repair. I'd say within the last year."

"Jane did mention that Oddjob had done some things around here. This is probably his work."

Patrea inspected the joined wood more closely. "I've seen worse. The place definitely needs windows, which is a huge expense, and this really is a lot of house for one person. It needs a family."

We spent a good hour puttering around from room to room while she detailed plans for the work she would do. From the sounds of things, the restoration and renovation process wouldn't be cheap, and wasn't location, location, location a thing?

"It sounds like a spendy project. Are you sure the sale price on the finished house will earn back the costs? This is Mooselick River, not Portland or even Bangor. Aren't you afraid of pricing yourself out of the local market?"

"It'll sell."

I should have known better than to even ask. She'd been taken over by the lure of fulfilling a dream. "I hope so. Are you ready to go? I have to meet Jacy soon."

"Just one more minute." Eyes alight with fervent glee, Patrea spun into a hip-shaking series of dance moves. "I'm just so happy. Take me to Jane and her mother. I want to make an offer."

Which is exactly what she did, one that brought tears to Jane's eyes and a smile to her mother's face.

CHAPTER TWENTY-TWO

When I pulled up to the back door of Curated Collections, Jacy was sitting on the top step. She pointed to her watch and gave me a look.

"Yes, I know I'm late," I said. "But let me tell you why." Before she could work up a full head of irritation, I told her about Patrea's impulsive purchase.

"Fine, you're off the hook." Jacy rarely stayed mad for more than a minute or two, but she wasn't above minor acts of revenge. "But I should probably warn you. I told my mom you were in the market for an essential oil fertility blend."

She headed for her car since she'd declared she would be driving.

"You did not." I followed her.

Jacy shrugged. "You're going to marry that man and give him babies. It's only a matter of time. Might as well be prepared."

"I distinctly remember telling you marriage was off the table for me."

"Spare me the once bitten routine. I'm not buying it anymore. You made a mistake with Paul. Own it.

He was a jerk, and you didn't see it. It happens. You rectified your error, took back your life and found one of the good ones. Way I see it, you made the best use of your learning experience, so why not enjoy the benefits? Marry the man. Have the pretty babies so I can play auntie and spoil them like you spoil Wade."

A pretty thought until you added ghosts to the mix.

"Screw that!" Jacy's exclamation made me realize I'd spoken out loud. "You...no, not just you...we have helped how many souls find peace even when it puts us in danger? You're nuts if you think any child you'd raise would be less than proud of you for helping someone, whether dead or alive."

Nothing like cutting right to the heart of the thing.

"I hear you. I do." It was time to change the subject. "Hey, that's new." I hadn't been out to visit Momma Wade in a while, and so the addition that doubled the size of her garden shed came as a surprise.

"She talked dad into building her a bigger drying shed since she's planning to expand her inventory if she takes over Davina's shop."

"If? I didn't know that was even a question."

With her beds tucked away for the winter, some under mulch, others under folding wooden frames stretched with burlap, Leandra's gardens still looked like something from a fairytale. I envied her green thumbs.

"You didn't hear the latest? She and Davina have had a

falling out from beyond the grave. I figured Davina would have told you by now."

News to me. "Davina was too preoccupied with haunting Martha to stop in for a gossip session. But now that I think about it, the Halloween event is over, and she hasn't been around much. I guess I figured she was hanging out here, but if she and Leandra are on the outs, maybe not. She popped in the other day to talk about Jober. I wonder if that's where she's been."

And did I really want to know?

Shrugging, Jacy held the gate open for me. "On this week's episode of Lifestyles of the Dead but not Departed, we have the Mystery of the Misplaced Mystic."

Funny.

A sad commentary on my life but funny all the same.

"Works in our favor, I suppose," I said to Jacy's back as I followed her toward the house. "I don't think Davina's going to be happy when she finds out we snooped through her stuff looking for her deepest, darkest secret."

"Probably less annoyed than she will be when she learns we found it."

"Don't remind me." Given her performance in the town office storage shed, Davina had figured out she could move things in the physical world if she wanted to badly enough. Since mine was the house that would be redecorated with her wrath, I'd rather put off that particular problem for as long as possible.

Except we were here to talk to Leandra about Davina's

pregnancy, so while the cat was still technically in the bag, I was holding scissors to the drawstring. If we didn't learn anything useful from Jacy's mom, I'd have to broach the subject with Davina myself anyway.

Inside the door, I took a deep breath. As usual, the house smelled like it had been seasoned by a generous cook. I recognized basil, rosemary, thyme, parsley, and lavender hanging from hooks above pots of those same herbs over-wintering on the deep kitchen windowsill. In place of curtains, thick braids of garlic and onions dangled down either side of the window, their earthy scents adding to the homey ambiance in the room.

Leandra must have heard us pull in because the teapot was already on, and she was just setting a plate of cookies that would probably taste a lot better than they looked on the table.

"Hi, Mom." Jacy went in for a hug and got a kiss on the cheek, but when I went to follow suit, Leandra turned away. When Jacy shot me a raised eyebrow, I wracked my memory, found nothing that could have put me on Momma Wade's bad side, and shrugged. Probably Davina's fault.

Leandra's fascination with the esoteric had been all-consuming until her deep desire to see a ghost came true and she discovered being haunted wasn't all she'd thought it would be. It was more, and she hadn't been prepared.

And yet, since she'd been the one with the whip and

the top hat, I would always maintain that this ghost thing *was* her circus, and Davina *was* her monkey. Had Leandra not dabbled with spirit guides and other things she didn't understand, my latent psychic ability wouldn't have been triggered, and by extension, she wouldn't be plagued with a spectral house guest.

Glancing at Jacy's belly, Leandra gave her daughter a questioning look.

"Not yet," Jacy laid a hand where she hoped there would soon be new life forming. "Still trying."

"That's half the fun." Leandra made her daughter blush.

"Are you alone?" I asked, even though there was no sign of Davina.

"I don't know. I can only see her when she's talking, and since we are no longer on speaking terms, I have no idea. She could be standing right behind me for all I know."

Shaking my head, I said, "She's not. I'm a little worried about her. I haven't seen much of her lately."

"Lucky you." As gentle a woman as you'd ever meet, Leandra could still spit venom-laced sarcasm like a pro and did not hesitate to do so when she thought the occasion warranted. Still, she added a scoop of my favorite tea into a mesh strainer and poured hot water over it, so I assumed most of her present attitude had more to do with Davina than with me.

"Okay." Jacy added enough honey to her cup that just

watching her do it made my teeth ache. "I have to know what Davina did to piss you off."

A moment passed while Leandra stirred half a spoonful of honey into her tea, sipped, and closed her eyes in bliss. Then, she said, "She has the sense of humor of a twelve-year-old."

Enlightening, but not the whole story. Jacy whirled a hand in the air to indicate her mother should elaborate.

After another sip of tea, Leandra said, "She wouldn't stop putting her finger in my tea."

The simple statement was enough to give me the whole picture, but Jacy frowned. "I don't get it. Wouldn't it just go right through? She's not like solid or anything, right?"

"No, but she's cold. Ghosts carry this otherworldly chill with them. You must have felt it when we were on the cliff that day."

"That's what that was?" Jacy seemed surprised. "I just figured my fear chilled me to the bone."

I shook my head. "Not entirely. So putting her finger in hot tea would—"

"She knows I don't like cold tea, but she thinks it's funny," Leandra interrupted me, then shot her daughter a glare when Jacy couldn't hold back a grin.

"The ghost version of a Wet Willie."

Since I'd had a ghost stick their finger in my ear once, I could say without hesitation that the two experiences would not be that similar. But it was probably best if I did something to diffuse the situation.

"You know, Davina's probably feeling a bit like her life—or rather, her death—is out of her control. She's stuck between worlds and has to depend on a perfect stranger to help her move forward. Ernie's doing the best he can, but with two deaths on his plate and the recent unpleasantness, he's stretched to the limit, and I've run out of suspects. In fact, that's what we've come here to talk to you about. But if you're mad at her and don't want her to go into the light, I guess we wasted our time."

I channeled my mother's chiding tone, but that couldn't be helped.

Properly chastened, Leandra caved. "Of course, I want her to go into the light."

"Given the sensitive nature of what we found, I think it's probably better if Davina's not here right now, anyway." Jacy chose a second cookie, broke off a piece, and dunked it in her tea. She made a valid point.

"What?" Curious now, Leandra leaned forward. "Tell me." Annoyed as she might be, this was a woman who loved with her whole heart. I felt a stab of guilt for making her feel bad before.

"What do you know about Davina's son?"

Her mouth dropping open and her brow furrowing into a frown gave me all the answers I needed. "You didn't know."

Leandra shook her head as if to clear away cobwebs,

then sat back in her chair, her eyes unfocused. She stayed still for at least two minutes, then shook her head again.

"Son?"

Jacy called up the photo of the adoption paperwork on her phone, and handed it over to her mother, who scanned it, then frowned harder.

"No. I didn't know, but now that I do," Leandra flicked the end of her braided hair behind her back and raised her voice loud enough to practically shake the rafters. "Lucy, you got some 'splainin' to do." Rising, she stalked across the room, opened a cabinet, and began to root through the rows of glass bottles while muttering to her spirit guide for help with what to choose.

"Dittany, aconite, and wormwood. Yes, that makes sense."

Jacy's eyes went wide at the use of Davina's true name and the tone in her mother's voice, which was not exactly welcoming. If I wasn't mistaken, Momma Wade was fixing to get her hoodoo on. I clapped a hand over my forehead when she grabbed her incense bowl and a hunk of dried cedar needles. The last time she'd mixed oils and ashes in my presence had not ended well for me. A second round was not on my menu.

"Lucille Bennet. Come. Now." It was not a request but a command delivered eerily enough to send a shiver across my skin. Jacy's, too, if her shudder meant anything.

"You've got a lot of nerve," Davina thundered as she shimmered into view.

"Whoa." Jacy pushed back her chair as if to get up and leave but stayed seated when her mother flashed her a quelling look. Apparently, we'd opened a can of worms. Or maybe something worse, like bees or scorpions.

"Who do you think you are to summon me without so much as a please or thank you?" To punctuate her outrage, Davina reached over and poked her finger into Leandra's cup. A skim of ice formed over the top of the recently-warm liquid.

"I've finished with it anyway," Leandra waved a hand. "And if you don't have something really good to say for yourself, I'm finished with you as well."

Hands on hips, Davina cocked her head and fixed her friend with a look that made more than the tea go cold. I shivered, and so did Jacy. "What is your problem?"

"Tell me about the baby."

In the movies, ghosts are usually pale, bleached-out versions of how they looked when they were alive. In the real world, they mostly look like living people, only they hover when they move, and you can't touch them, so when I say Davina went white, I mean it in the sense of going pale just like anyone does when they've had bad news. She clutched the collar of her blouse.

"How did you find out about him?"

Crap. Busted. Might as well own it. "I told her," I said, my voice quavering as the feet of my chair lifted slightly off the floor. "You weren't giving me anything to work with, so I went to your house and looked around for something to help figure out who would want to kill you. I was only trying to help."

"We," Jacy cut in. "I was there, too. So you might as well be mad at both of us."

"Bzz." Davina clapped together the fingers and thumb of her right hand in a gesture that was clearly intended to shut Jacy up.

Didn't work. I could have predicted as much.

"Did you just buzz at me?" Color rising, Jacy sucked in a breath to say something else, but I reached over and pinched her arm. Hard. "Ouch."

If she didn't shut up, things could get ugly. Or we were already past the tipping point for that. I wasn't sure. Just like I wasn't sure what was behind all the subtext between the ghost and the older woman, but it was definitely there. Smarter all the way around to just sit back and let them hash it out. Still, I slid my chair closer to Jacy's. She was a mom with a baby at home, and if the furniture started flying, I was ready to throw myself in front of her for protection.

"Who's the father?" Ignoring us, Leandra demanded.

Davina sighed. "Does it really matter anymore? I did the right thing by my boy." She didn't sound convinced, but having been faced with one of the hardest decisions a woman could make, she'd probably spent years second-guessing herself.

"It does to me. It would to my husband and to my

kids. If they have a half-brother out there somewhere, they deserve to know."

"A who in the what, now?" Jacy half stood, but I yanked her back down while possibilities spun circles in my head.

"Your father dated Lucy for a few weeks during their senior year of high school. This would be," Leandra's eyes flicked upward as she did the math in her head. "A couple of months before she took off. We now know she was pregnant when she left. So...I want to know if he's the father."

Well, that explained what had crawled up Leandra's backside.

"Did I get hit on the head, and now I'm dreaming I'm in a soap opera?" Jacy leaned over and whispered in my ear. That it was a reasonable question made the moment even more surreal.

"No. Oh, Lee. No. I'm sorry I didn't tell you, but that's not why." The fight had gone out of the ghost. "I've been so ashamed."

Leandra heaved a relieved sigh, as did Jacy. I couldn't blame them. A mystery half-brother would have been a lot to take. "Tell me now. Please. I think we'll both feel better if you do."

Davina nodded but didn't launch right into her tale. Instead, she hover-paced while she tried to find the words.

"First, I knew that boy wasn't for me after just a few dates. He was a very nice young man. Solid. Dependable."

"Boring?" A hint of a smile tugged at the corners of Leandra's mouth.

"I didn't say that. Not at all." All earnestness now, Davina came to the table, sat in the chair Leandra automatically pulled out for her. "I had this restlessness inside me, which I now know had more to do with my work than my love life, but at the time, I wanted danger."

Dangerous wouldn't appear on anyone's list of words describing Jacy's dad. Kind, loving, constant, silly, generous, and tolerant would. He'd have done the right thing by Davina if he'd been the father of her son.

"You didn't." Leandra's eyes went wide.

"I did." Davina nodded. "And I got caught out for my sins."

"Okay, I have to ask. Did the…uh…book match up to the cover?"

Jacy rolled her eyes. "I'm officially horrified by this discussion, but mostly because that was the lamest euphemism on the planet. Who was this guy?"

While Davina looked away, Leandra explained. "I was two grades behind Lucy in school and so desperate to fit in with the older crowd that I made her take me to some of their sandpit parties."

"Oh, just call it like it was, Lee. These weren't parties, they were mad drinking binges with music and unlikely couples groping in the bushes."

"I didn't do any drinking or groping," Leandra assured her daughter. "Not that year, anyway. I didn't know it at the time, but I was waiting for your father. He was my first and such a gentle lover."

Jacy stuck her fingers in her ears. "Too much information. Just stop. I beg of you. Let Davina tell her story before I turn to stone or something."

"There's not much to tell, really. It's a classic story, old as time. Naive girl meets leather-clad hooligan and can't see past the stars in her eyes. He told me I was special and he'd never met anyone like me. Blah, blah. I fell for all the standard lines, and under a full moon on a chilly night at the beginning of May, I let him take me on a dirty wool blanket. I can still remember how the wool smelled and the noises he made while he forever changed my life."

All the humor drained from the moment. Leandra reached over to pat her friend on the hand and winced when hers dropped through the chill to the table below. "I wish you'd have told me at the time. I'd have been there for you."

"I wanted to, and then, by the time I found out I was pregnant, he was long gone, and I realized I didn't even know his real name. He was just some guy that rolled into town, stayed a couple of weeks, and then rolled back out."

My tea had gone cold, but I took a sip of it anyway and said, "But you knew where to find him, didn't you? I mean, given what you do...did for a living, you'd have known where to look."

She shrugged. "I bought a home pregnancy test and got my results on graduation day. The next morning, I packed a bag and hitched a ride to Bangor. Grabbed the first bus leaving Maine and ended up at a shelter in Trenton, New Jersey. They helped me get a job, connected me with an adoption agency, and even offered counseling to help me cope with the decision to give up the baby."

"I never knew." Leandra knuckled a tear from her cheek as sympathy laced her voice. "It must have been so hard."

"It was the best thing I could do for my son. I never doubted that for a moment. It was a closed adoption, not so I wouldn't be tempted to go looking for him later because I didn't need names on a piece of paper for that, but so he couldn't come looking for me."

The question popped out before I could stop it, and I regretted asking almost before it left my lips. "Is that why you never married? Didn't you want more children?"

Davina closed her eyes for a long moment.

"I'm sorry. I shouldn't have asked."

"No, it's okay. I've been holding onto this secret for so long it's colored my entire life. Giving up my son was the thing that made me want to hone my skills. I needed to gain control. Mostly so I could close off the piece of me that wanted to find him, still the voice in my head that insisted it couldn't hurt to just know. It wouldn't have stopped there because once I found him, it wouldn't take long to convince myself it was okay to go and look at him. Just once. From a distance.”

By now, Leandra wasn't the only teary-eyed person in the room, and it was about to get worse.

“There were complications, you see. With the birth, I mean. I'll spare you the technical jargon, but there would be no more babies for me.”

At that point, Momma Wade let out an actual sob.

“Don't,” Davina ordered. “Don't you dare feel sorry for me. Despite my maudlin tale, I've had a good life, and I trust that my son did as well. So stop sniveling, or you'll piss me off. I don't want your pity or anyone's, which is why I have worked hard at keeping my private life out of the public eye. And don't, for one minute, think my life was lonely or loveless just because I never wanted to shackle myself to one man for the whole of it. Variety is the spice of life, you know.”

As she began to fade around the edges, Davina fixed Leandra with a half-smile and held up her bent pinkie finger. “To answer your earlier question, the cover definitely was better than the book, if you know what I mean. In fact, he gave new meaning to the term *put a sock in it*.”

Her eyes still a bit watery, Leandra returned the smile. “I'm not surprised.”

“But,” Davina's smile widened to a full-on grin as she named a popular soap opera actor. “Let's just say that man could put a whole drawer full of socks to shame.” She waggled her fingers and then faded out completely.

"Again," Jacy's tone was drier than her favorite wine, "too much information."

Or maybe not enough, but I was thinking more of murder than scandal, and nothing Davina had revealed seemed remotely helpful. She didn't know where her son was, hadn't revealed the father's name—or maybe she hadn't known it. I could ask Leandra later, but I was still paddling in the shallow end of the suspect pool.

Jacy said as much on the drive back home. "The closed adoption pretty much rules out the father, the son, and the new family."

"Not necessarily." I had already cued up the browser on my phone to run a search. "From what I see here, there's a mutual consent registry, but Davina would have to sign up for that to work. Based on what she told us, I doubt she did. Then there are detective services dedicated to adoption."

"What about those DNA testing places? You hear about people finding distant relatives on those all the time."

I pointed to my phone. "Yeah, it's on the list, but there again, that all depends on someone from the birth family having sent in a sample, and I doubt Davina did."

"Right," Jacy took one hand off the wheel to wave it practically in my face. "But it doesn't have to be her, does it? I think it would work the same if anyone in her family did."

"Stop weaving all over the road, and I'll check."

"I'm not weaving. I'm merely dodging potholes to save wear and tear on my suspension." So saying, she whipped around a particularly large one. "This road took a beating last winter."

"You could warn a person before you do that." I rubbed my arm where it had slammed against the door and went back to reading options for bypassing closed adoptions.

"Pothole," Jacy yelled, scaring me half out of my skin. "There, don't say I didn't warn you." She yanked the wheel left, and I had to grab the door handle.

"Next time, I'm driving," I growled.

"You want me to stop at the hardware store so you can talk to Tim Bennet?"

I shook my head. "How would that go? Hey, Tim. You know that sister you just lost? Well, here's a bombshell. She had a baby and didn't tell anyone. How do I know? Um...I broke into her house and rifled through her stuff because her ghost is an uncooperative pain in my backside."

"Okay. I get that. It's complicated."

"More than," I tucked my phone back into my purse and took a moment to think out loud. "I'm assuming there's more to the process than sending in a sample and getting an email with a list of people who match. It's a privacy thing."

"True, and if the son had anything to do with Davina's death, he'd have had to make contact with whoever did send in their DNA so they'd know who to target before she was killed. Someone gets hold of me to say they're my long-lost cousin or nephew or whatever, I'm not keeping that to myself."

A fair point. "Agreed."

"Then we're thinking it probably didn't happen, right?"

"Seems like it. I mean, someone would have said something, and according to Davina, she didn't have a lot of extended family, so this looks like another dead end."

The only good thing to come from the visit was that the drama had driven all thoughts of fertility oil from Leandra's mind, so I had that going for me.

CHAPTER TWENTY-THREE

"Check-in begins at eleven and ends at five. You can lock up at five on the dot since most people are fine with self-checkout. There's a key box by the door. You already know my sister will be here on Friday to take over for the weekend, so I'll only need you for two days." Barbara's fingers shook a little when she put her hand on my arm. "If anyone shows up, you've got Miranda's number for cleaning, and the wi-fi password is in that top drawer in case you need to reset the system. Sometimes it acts up."

"Do you mean Miranda Perkins?" Server at Cappy's.

"Miranda's filling in for my regular housekeeper who took time off to tend to her mother after a knee replacement. The arrangement has worked well for both of us since the bar will be closed until the police have cleared it to open back up."

Made sense to me.

"I've got this. You go see that baby, and don't worry about a thing." I put my hand over hers and gave it a squeeze.

"I'm not worried. It's the quiet season, and we have no

bookings, so I expect you're in for a boring couple of days." She winked at me. "There's a box under the counter with some stimulating reading material should you have any interest."

"Good to know." I had to work to keep from grinning. "I brought my laptop to keep me busy."

"Okay." Her sigh gusted. "If you have questions about the new computer booking system, just call my sister. Her number is on that sheet I gave you. Or you can probably grab any eleven-year-old kid off the street, and they'll figure it out for you."

"Don't worry about a thing," I repeated. "I've got this. Give that baby a kiss on the cheek for me." As Jacy had pointed out, I did eventually want babies. Living with Drew was going well enough that I thought I might be ready to start thinking about maybe starting a family at some point. How's that for being decisive? Until "some point" became now, I'd have to settle for giving Jacy's son, Wade, a cuddle every chance I got.

"Okay." Seeming calmer, Barbara picked up her purse and headed for the door. "If I don't leave now, I'll be late. Thanks for doing this."

I waved her out and looked around the unit converted into an office where I knew Barb sometimes slept if the weather was bad at closing time. In true motel style, the office featured a scaled-down version of all the comforts of home. The sofa facing the small TV mounted on the wall looked comfortable enough for sitting or sleeping.

The combination sink and refrigerator plus a two-burner hotplate allowed for cooking a basic meal, and best of all, Barb didn't mind me bringing my dog along. There were worse places to work for a day or two.

While I completed my tour of the office, Molly stared longingly at the swath of grass between the parking lot and the main road.

"You want a game of fetch, girl?" I asked the foolish question to which the answer was always yes and watched Molly shiver in anticipation. "Give me one minute to set the phone system to forward to my cell in case anyone calls, and then we can go out for a bit."

Dogs are supposed to understand quite a few words and concepts, but wait one minute is not Molly's favorite phrase. She danced in place the entire time it took me to scan the directions for the phone system.

"Walk with me." We'd been working on off-leash commands, which Molly picked up like a champ. As eager as she was, she practically plastered herself to my side during the walk across the parking lot. "Okay, get ready." That was her cue. She took off across the grass, spun, and waited for me to throw the ball, her body quivering with such delight I couldn't hold back a smile.

We played a good twenty minutes before my cell phone rang with a call forwarded from the office.

"Bide-A-Way, how can I help you?"

The man on the other end of the line sounded tired. "How many rooms do you have available?"

A good question. I turned and counted. "Seven."

"I'll take them."

So much for a quiet couple of days at the motel. "All of them?"

"Is that a problem?"

"No. Of course, not. Can I have your name, please?"

"Just book them under the company name. JBL Tours. I've got thirty people on a broken-down bus that can't be fixed until tomorrow, no way to get a replacement here in time, and the only motel for miles has just seven rooms. That's great." It sounded like he was talking to himself rather than me.

"We have seven rooms here and a couple of extra cots, so we can easily take as many as seventeen if people don't mind sharing. Then, there's the Marlow. Right in the heart of town, it's more of a bed and breakfast type thing, but I know the owner, and they have room for the rest. I can make a call and set that up for you."

A sigh whispered across the line. "Really? That would be fantastic. I don't suppose you know the number for the local taxi...if there even is one. We're at some hole-in-the-wall garage called Pine Tree Automotive, and I need to get a bus full of people from here to there."

I took pity on him.

"Give me ten minutes, and I'll see what I can do to help." I took his number and promised to call right back, then hung up and dialed the inn.

"We've got a situation," I explained when David

answered, then gave him the rundown. "I'm working on transportation next. I'll text you when I have things settled." My next call was to Martha.

"A bus full of tourists? What on earth are they doing here at this time of year? The leaves are down, and we're not exactly in the most scenic of seasons."

"Does it really matter?"

"I guess not." I could almost hear the wheels turning in her head. Tourists meant money. "I can have Willie Mason drive out to Bennie's garage with a school bus in twenty minutes or less."

"That's perfect. I've got David on standby for the rest of the rooms, and I'll call Mabel and ask her to pass the word to House of Pizza and Bertie's to expect a run on delivery orders."

Martha practically hummed. "What if we also had Willie pull in one of the smaller buses for shuttle service?"

That would work. "Sounds good to me. I'll call the driver back and let him know what we've put together. Good work, Martha."

And don't get any ideas about throwing together an event of some sort. I kept that last to myself and hung up before she could. When I called the bus driver back, he couldn't have been more grateful.

"This is how we do things here in Mooselick River," I told him. "Hang tight. Your ride will be along soon. Call back if you need anything, and in the meantime, I'll set up the extra cots."

Because warning her seemed like a good idea, I also called Miranda Perkins.

"I can come out right now if you need help with the cots," she offered. "I'm less than ten minutes away."

And give me a chance to talk to her about Jober Peavey? Sure.

"That would be fantastic. We'll have a full house here in under an hour, so I'll take all the help I can get."

"On my way."

In the meantime, I grabbed the master key and checked all the rooms to make sure we truly were ready. When Miranda pulled in, I was just dragging the first cot out of the storage area.

"It's always something, isn't it?" Miranda said, her tone more cheerful than annoyed.

"Seems like it." I hated to bring up painful topics, but I didn't have to because Miranda beat me to it.

"I'm glad to have this extra work, but if Cappy's doesn't open back up, I'm not sure what I'll do."

"Is that a possibility?"

"If Milo gets arrested, I'm sure his wife will close the place."

Frowning, I qualified, "Wait, does Milo own the bar? I thought he just worked there."

Face flushing, Miranda clapped a hand over her mouth. "No one's supposed to know. You won't say anything, will you?"

I shook my head, my mystery-solving senses beginning to tingle. "Cross my heart."

"Okay. And it will all probably come out now that Milo's in trouble, but a few months ago, the owners decided to sell and contacted a national chain to see if they were interested in making an offer. They declined, by the way, because the town's too small to generate enough revenue. When Milo got wind of the opportunity to buy Cappy's, he took out a second mortgage on his place to cover the down payment."

Just one more reason why it made no sense for him to commit murder on the premises. Not only would getting caught cost his freedom, but the scandal could lose Milo both his business and his house.

"Do you know what Jober had against Milo? He certainly threatened a lot of people with airing their dirty laundry the night he died." After her conversation with Jacy, Miranda had gone off the shortlist, but then again, she'd held back the news about Milo owning the bar, so maybe we'd removed her too early.

She'd taken one side of the foldaway bed while I grabbed the other.

"Jacy asked me about that, too, and I'll tell you the same thing I told her. Milo was the only person in town who genuinely listened to Oddjob when he got going with his stories. Yarns. That's what Milo called them. Load of BS mostly, if you ask me."

Together, we wrestled the first cot into place and went back for the second before I raised the topic again.

"I've heard a few of Oddjob's stories since his untimely death, and there were some doozies."

"Tell me about it. Did you hear the one about your mother?"

Surprise slowed my steps. "No. Do I want to know?"

"It wasn't his worst one by any stretch of the imagination, but I'm pretty sure she's not a CIA operative sent to town to spy on people by reporting what books they like to read."

I couldn't hold back the snort or the laugh. "No. She's not. I wonder where he got that idea."

"Pulled it out of his ass, most likely."

We popped the second cot into place and went back for the last of the three. "There's usually a kernel of truth in even the most farfetched stories," I said. "I can't figure out what that one would be, though."

"Hah," Miranda gave me a grin. "I can. I'm betting she recommended a book he might like. She does that for me sometimes, and she's always right, by the way. Probably Jober wasn't happy to hear someone knew what brand of filth he liked to read."

Since several people had mentioned Oddjob's dirty mind, she'd probably nailed the reason.

"But you're right about the kernel of truth thing," Miranda handed me a set of bedding, took two more sets from the shelf. "Like, if I'm thinking about it, he probably did see me add water to a liquor bottle once. We keep a mix of grain alcohol, water, and lemon essential oil on hand for cleaning purposes."

"Let me guess, you got the recipe from Leandra Wade."

"Bingo. Works like a charm, too. I heard she's taking over Davina Benet's shop. I'm hoping she stocks more of her own stuff if she does. Her bug-bite balm is the next best thing to magic, and I need to stock up on her flu tonic in case it's bad again this year."

Leandra might have screwed up my life with her oils and ashes, but I still loved her like family, so hearing such high praise made me smile. "Thanks for reminding me. I'll need to do the same."

I grabbed extra toiletries for the rooms with cots while Miranda went for extra towels and, while I still had her in a chatty mood, asked if she knew Jober's dinner companion from the night of his death.

"Oh sure, that was Mrs. McCarthy. She's one of his odd jobs."

"How so?"

Miranda shrugged. "She doesn't drive. Like never had a license at all. Bad eyesight, I think. I only know her husband did all the driving until he passed. After that, she got hooked up with Jober."

"Hooked up?" I tried hard not to let my mind go where it wanted to go with that.

"Ew. Not like that. She's eighty years old." Miranda

shuddered. "He ran errands for her, took her to appointments, and once a month to dinner. That kind of thing. I hope she can find someone to take his place."

And she probably wasn't physically capable of murdering him, either. So that was one more suspect off the list.

"What about Adam? How well do you know him?"

"Well enough to know he didn't kill Jober Peavey." Miranda shifted her grip on the sheets and towels.

"But he did kill someone?"

Miranda jolted. "How did you hear about that?"

I could have thrown Robin under the bus, but I didn't. "I'm not sure. Someone mentioned it in passing."

"It was an accident." Miranda shook her head. Sorrow crept into her tone. "He told me about it one night when we were working late. A carload of teenagers going just a little too fast. Add a patch of loose gravel, and you've got the makings of a tragedy. Adam was driving."

Because I could picture it, I shuddered. "That's awful."

"He lost his best friend that night, and he's never forgiven himself. He doesn't drive, either, by the way. Not since that night. Or not cars, anyway. He rides a bicycle to work during the summer, and one of us gives him a ride home when it's cold."

"Who took him home last Friday?" My crime-solving senses began to tingle.

"Milo."

Splitting off, Miranda made up the first cot while I did

the second, then joined me to work together on the third. While she hadn't been a fount of knowledge, she'd helped me see a point I'd missed before. All we had to do was find the right kernel of truth in one of Jober's wild stories, and maybe, if we were lucky, it would lead us to his killer.

Not that I had time to spend thinking about murder for the next couple of hours. I was too busy getting the tourists settled in for the night. Miranda left as soon as the rooms were ready and promised to come back the next day to clean rooms.

CHAPTER TWENTY-FOUR

*M*olly raced ahead of me to bark at the front door while I hauled my weary body up the steps. Drew wasn't supposed to be home yet, so when his distorted face popped up behind the wavy glass panel, I would have cheered if I had the energy for it.

When he opened the door, and the smell of pepperoni and Bertino's special sauce wafted out, I found the energy for a half-hearted whoop.

"You're home early." Sliding into Drew's arms was the best part of my day.

"You're home late." He kissed me on the top of my head. "Guess we both had a weird day."

"Tell me about yours." I followed him to the kitchen, grabbed a glass of ice water, and filled Molly's food bowl. "Pizza was a genius move, by the way."

Drew held up a hand. "Don't give me credit for that one. The delivery guy showed up here two minutes before you did with a free pie and breadsticks. Wouldn't take a tip, either, and when I asked why, said you'd know."

He'd set the table with a minimum of niceties, which didn't bother me one bit. My butt barely hit the chair before I whipped open the pizza box and grabbed the nearest slice.

"Extra cheese, too." Closing my eyes, I sank my teeth into sheer heaven. "I needed that. And I'll warn you, if your masculine sensibilities are likely to be offended by a woman eating her weight in pizza, you should look away now."

Grinning, Drew chose a slice and grated a generous dusting of Parmesan on top. "Whatever gets you through the day, darling."

"Barbara didn't even make it to the airport before chaos hit. A tour bus broke down, and they couldn't get a replacement before tomorrow, which is when Bennie will have it fixed anyway. So we have a full house at the motel —I'm on standby, by the way—and the inn's at capacity."

"Not sure I'm getting the nuance that resulted in free pizza, but I am grateful."

"Oh, I called every eating establishment in town and coordinated getting the tourists fed, and fed well. The tour company covered the cost, and the tourists were happy enough to tip well. It seems this little side trip is giving them a first-hand look at small-town life. My phone's been blowing up with messages. They went to town—literally—and spent wads of cash in the craft shops."

"Which, if I know you, you prevailed upon the owners to stay open late."

"I did do that, as a matter of fact." I waved my slice at

him. "You know, it galls me to admit it, but Martha is right. Getting more tourists to detour into Mooselick River would be good for the town. We need something to draw in more buses like this one."

We tangled feet under the table. "Your wheels are already turning."

"I can't help it. I'm just wired that way." The worst of my hunger sated, I chose a breadstick and dipped it in marinara. "Plus, if I don't find an alternative solution, Martha has some wild ideas she's likely to put in motion. I really don't think we need to become the next Salem. Even if we had the history to back that up, which we don't."

Drew tilted his head while he considered. "Hackinaw has the lake, so they're pulling in the outdoor types, and the resort serves those who'd rather see nature mostly through glass."

"Right." I nodded. "Plus, there's all the boutique shopping. We can't compete with any of that, and really, we don't want to. We do have our end of the lake and a few cabin rentals, but nothing wide-scale, which I think is a good thing."

"Probably," Drew agreed.

"If I've learned anything today, it's that we aren't ready for a lot of overnight guests yet, so we should probably concentrate on scooping up day-trippers for a start. I think if we pushed the craft/art/antique shopping angle, we could get some of these tour buses to add us as a short stop along the way."

I remembered his earlier comment about having a weird day. "But enough of that. What was your weird day like?"

He kept his face carefully blank. "I had a visitor at work."

In my world, *weird* and *visitor* combined into *ghost.* Since Drew had become part of my world, he was subject to the same, and since I couldn't think of a better option, I asked, "Davina?"

"How did you guess?" The question was rhetorical, but I didn't sense annoyance coming from him, which was good because until Davina passed through the veil and closed the door behind her, weird would keep happening.

"What did she want? I think she's been avoiding me since the haunting of Martha debacle."

Also, why did she go to him and not me? Was I jealous? I hoped not but didn't want to plumb the depths of that question for several reasons.

"She wasn't alone."

"You have got to be kidding me." I took the last two slices, slipped one on my plate, and one on Drew's, flipped the cover on the empty pizza box, and sat back in my chair to wait for the story, which promised to be interesting.

"If only I were." Drew tapped his fingers on the table a few times. "Do you have any idea how annoying it is when there's a ghost buzzing in your ear while you're trying to carry on a conversation with someone living?"

I could not keep the sarcasm from my answer. "No. I

wouldn't have a clue. Do tell." He'd just described my life for more than a year.

Drew tossed me a thousand-yard stare that lasted only a moment before he relented and quirked a smile. "Okay, I guess you probably do have some experience in that area."

"It helps if you cover your mouth and pretend to cough. Not a lot because if you do it often enough, people think there's something wrong with you."

His smile widened. I loved that he found humor in the same things I did. "Probably not as much as if they catch you talking to thin air a lot."

He got it.

"Next time one of us sees her, we'll have to remind her to use proper ghost decorum from here on out. What did she want, and who was with her?" It could only be one of two people. Or one person, I supposed, and one ghost. Seeing Leandra wouldn't have put that look on his face.

"Never mind. It had to be Jober. Could you see him, too?"

Soberly, Drew nodded. "Clear as day. He didn't look so good, either. Davina says he's suffering from something she called deadly denial, and if we can't get through to him before it's time, he might not cross over into the light."

"By we, you mean me." Of course. "Except he's scared of me because he thinks I'm the ghost. She popped up the other day to mention something about Jober's state of mind, but I didn't think things sounded that dire."

Since it was empty, I flattened the box, shoved it into the recycling bin.

"Grab a bottle of wine. I'll get the glasses." So saying, I took the discussion into the living room, stepped over Molly's sprawled form, and settled with my feet on the coffee table. "I appreciate Davina trying to help, but I'm not sure why she thought she should drag you into the middle of this mess."

Drew snorted.

"I think because she'd already shown herself to me, it was easier to do the second time, and because he was adamant that he 'wasn't trusting his mortal soul in the hands of a woman'."

As dry as the wine was, it couldn't compare to my tone. "Sure. Because we don't bring life into this world or anything, what would we know about taking life out of it?"

Spinning to rest his feet on my lap, Drew assured, "You can be in charge of my soul anytime. It should be easy since you already have my heart."

"Smooth talker." He earned a foot rub.

"I have my moments." His feet came off my lap as he gently pulled me down to lie beside him, his lips taking mine in the sweetest of kisses. "Wanna practice bringing life into the world?"

"It does make perfect." He kissed me again, and in the pursuit of affirming life, I forgot about death for a while.

CHAPTER TWENTY-FIVE

A pale sun sparked crystal glitters across frost-coated grass that crunched under the boots I'd hastily pulled on to take Molly out for her morning romp. After a visit to her favorite corner of the yard, she raced up the back porch steps to grab the tennis ball launcher, then danced around near the gate.

"You want to go to the dog park before we clock in at the motel?" We hadn't been since I'd hurt my wrist, and I wasn't sure I could do the ball launcher justice with my left hand, but I couldn't resist the naked longing in her warm, brown eyes or the excited wiggle of her hind end. "Okay, give me five minutes to get dressed, and we'll go." I could grab coffee and a pastry at the Gas-N-Go after Molly had had her fun.

Five minutes must feel like an eternity to a dog, but Molly was as patient as she could manage and only yipped once to hurry me along. When I opened the door, she bounced into the back seat like her butt was made out of springs, then settled down for the short ride.

We turned left onto a dirt road lined with trees and

discovered the entrance to the park partially blocked by a dump truck with an empty trailer.

"Hang on, Molls." I guided old Sally between the ditch and the end of the trailer with about a whisper's room to spare, parked, and popped open the rear door. A sleek, brown bullet, she launched toward the gate, dropped to her haunches, and waited for me to catch up.

If my left-handed ball launching skills weren't up to par, Molly didn't seem to care as she ran full-out, snatched the ball out of the air, and raced back to drop it at my feet. Her tongue lolling, her doggy eyes alight with the thrill of the chase, she played for twenty minutes before heading back to the gate to wait for me.

"I guess you're done, then." And in need of a drink. I got out her portable dish and filled it from the faucet near the gate.

"If you come back tomorrow, you'll have to bring your own. I'll shut the water off today, so it doesn't freeze over the winter."

I recognized Brian's cousin Vernon as he walked around the front corner of the dump truck that I now realized belonged to him. What an excellent piece of timing. The universe was looking out for me.

"Thanks for letting me know."

"You probably don't remember me," he said.

"Sure I do. You're Dibble French."

A huge grin split his round and earnest face. "Nobody calls me that anymore."

"I'm sorry. I didn't mean anything by it."

A meaty hand waved away the apology. "Don't worry about it. I'm sure no one calls you Everly Beverly anymore, either."

"Nope." I grinned back at him because the cheerful boy I remembered had grown into an equally cheerful man. "I haven't heard that one in years."

Having slurped her weight in water, Molly finally turned her attention to the humans, greeting Vernon with her best doggy smile and some frantic tail-wagging.

"Hi there, fella. What's your name?" Bending, he let her sniff his hand, and when she decided he passed muster, gave her the attention she craved. "Pretty dog. Looks like he's got a sweet disposition."

"Her name's Molly, and she does."

"Hello, Molly. It's nice to meet you." Straightening, Vernon leaned against the hood of my car as if getting comfortable. It seemed we would be catching up. Since I had an hour before I needed to be at the motel, I didn't mind a bit. At least it allowed me to wrangle the conversation around to Jober Peavey and his untimely death.

Leaning beside him, I stuck to the safe topics first, pointing to his name splashed across the door of the dump truck. "I heard you took over the business from your father. How are your folks doing?"

Vernie nodded. "Really well now, but it was rough those first few months after my mom's diagnosis. Watching her go through chemo was the worst, but she's been cancer-free for over a year. They'll be leaving for Arizona in a few days."

"Vacation?"

He shook his head. "Snowbirds. Mom couldn't take the winters here anymore, so as soon as she was cleared for travel, they bought an RV and headed south. Last year they went to Florida, but dad said it was too crowded for his taste, so this year, they headed west." He bumped my shoulder with his, "Saw the reports about your ex on the news."

I sighed. "Everyone did. Nothing like having your private life splashed all over the TV."

"Did you really find him chained to a bed?"

The number one question I still got asked. "Yep. I really did." Even now, the memory brought a certain amount of evil joy.

"Huh."

"What about you? Married? Kids?"

He reached for his wallet instead of his phone, pulled out a laminated photo taken at Christmas with his family, all in matching skiing penguin pajamas. "That's my wife, Doreen, and our two kids, Amos and Amanda." They looked happy.

"What a beautiful family," I said and meant the compliment sincerely. "Your son looks just like you."

"Poor kid," Vernie grinned again. "Did you know boys have birthday sleepovers these days? You'd think it was just a girl thing, but you'd be wrong. His birthday was a week ago last Friday. Wall to wall boys, very little actual sleeping involved, and we're still finding pizza crust in weird places."

Ding. Ding went the little bell in my head.

"A week ago Friday? Wasn't that the night Jober Peavey was killed?"

The smile fell off Vernon's face as he nodded. "We'd fed the birthday bunch and got them settled in front of a movie when my wife realized they'd eaten the pizza she set aside for us. She wasn't up to cooking, so she sent me over to Cappy's for takeout. I was still waiting when Ernie came in and arrested that lawyer woman." He pushed off from his relaxed position, paced a few steps, and then turned to face me.

"Is it true that Jober cost you a lucrative job?"

"Where did you hear that?"

I sensed no more than curiosity behind the question, and Vernie's gaze met mine squarely. A good thing because I didn't want him to be guilty of murder.

"Oh, word gets around." I refused to throw Bennie under the bus.

"It's true." He took off his ball cap, scratched his head, then put the hat back on. "But there's more to the story if you're interested."

I nodded and waved an encouraging hand.

"I put in a bid for repaving the parking lots for Pinewoods Health Center. To be honest, I didn't figure I'd get it anyway because they wanted all three locations done at the same time, and I'm not quite big enough of an outfit for that. But I figured I'd throw my hat in the ring, and if I got the job, I'd find a way to make it work."

"So it was a long shot before Jober got involved anyway?"

Vernon nodded. "The longest."

There went his motive.

"Listen, I felt sorry for the guy. You know his story, right?"

Somehow, I didn't think he meant the tall ones Jober liked to tell. "I guess not."

More relaxed now, Vernon took his earlier position leaning against my hood. "He lost his entire family in a house fire. That kind of grief, well, it does things to a man. He was convinced someone set the fire, but it was ruled accidental. I got no way of knowing for sure, but I figure that's what made him the way he was, so I cut him some slack. Family is everything to me, and I think it was the same for him."

A rush of sympathy welled up inside me.

"I've talked to a lot of people, and no one mentioned anything about Jober's family before." Mentally, I cursed myself for not thinking to look into Jober's past. He'd pissed off so many people in town that it hadn't occurred to me to dig any deeper than that.

"Probably didn't know. He didn't talk about his family at all, and I only found out when my wife brought the kids to one of the job sites. Mandy, my little girl, took one look at Jober and started crying."

"Scared of him?"

But Vernon shook his head. "Sad for him. 'That poor man has a broken heart,' she said, and she was right. Whole thing shook him up some. Enough to tell me what happened, and that was probably the only time I ever knew him to tell a straight story."

"One of those stories is probably what got him killed." Even though Vernon had bumped himself down to the bottom of my list, I watched for signs of prevarication, saw none.

"You're probably right. I felt sorry for the man, but that doesn't mean he wasn't twisted in the head. Working with him, I heard a few doozies."

That perked me up. "Anything that might pertain to his death?"

"Maybe." Vernon shrugged. "Hard to tell. You couldn't believe half of what he said about people." He rattled off the high points of the more salacious stories I'd already heard. "He had me going right up until the one where Mr. Herbert masterminded an attempt to rob the bank."

I almost choked on a laugh. "Mr. Herbert? You have got to be kidding me."

Solemnly, he shook his head. "Jober had no concept of the difference between fact and fiction."

"Clearly." The mental image of Mr. Herbert in a vault, dressed in black, readjusting his up-and-over hairstyle while dangling off the end of a rope admittedly came from watching too many movies, but it would haunt me for quite some time. I was still trying to shake it out of my head when Ernie Polk's cruiser crunched across the dead grass along the side of the road.

As usual, Ernie scowled when he saw me. I supposed I couldn't blame him, but I did.

"Everly," he said as he approached.

"Ernie." I mimicked his annoyed tone.

Then he turned his attention to Vernon, held up a bolt almost the diameter of a broom handle. "This what you needed?"

Stepping forward, Vernon took the bolt, ran his thumbnail over the threads. "Close enough, I'll wager, and thanks for dropping it off."

Affable as he never was with me, Ernie grinned. "No problem, I was headed out this way anyhow. You need a hand with anything?"

"Nah, I'm good. I'll just get back to work, then. Nice to see you again, Everly."

"Same goes," I said.

Vernon picked up the toolbox he'd left on the ground next to his truck. Whistling a tune, he headed off to fix whatever was broken.

Figuring it was the safest way to open the conversation, and because I genuinely wanted to know, I asked, "Any news on Milo?"

"He's through the worst of it. Should be going home today or tomorrow."

"Home," I picked up on the operative word. Ernie heaved a sigh.

"Yes. Home."

"Not the pokey, then?"

Ernie chopped the air with one hand. "It's official police business, but since I know you'll pry until you find out anyway, I'll tell you this much. None of the blood on Milo's hands or clothing belonged to Jober Peavey."

"That's great news."

"For Milo, sure. Doesn't help me much," Ernie said. "I've got the press breathing down my neck about Davina Benet, and I can't scare up a suspect. With Jober and his wild tales, half the town is on my list."

As if for comfort, Molly sidled up to Ernie, leaned against his leg, and let her tongue loll out when he reached down to give her a scratch behind the ears.

Because it was still a sore spot, I said, "I'm assuming my mother's not one of them. I know he thought she was a CIA agent sent here to spy on people through their choice of reading material, but that's not really a motive for murder."

Ernie just about choked.

"What? You hadn't heard that one?"

He shook his head, humor finally lighting his eyes. "No, I had not, but it certainly would explain a lot."

"I'll tell her you said so," I teased.

"I'd rather you didn't. I'm already on her bad side as it is."

"If it helps, she no longer adds the word jackass whenever she says your name," I said. "I'd say she's halfway to forgiving you. Tell her she's okay to leave town, then give it another week, and she'll be fine."

"Small mercies, I guess."

"I also heard Mr. Herbert tried to rob the bank."

Ernie threw his head back and laughed. "That one, I'd heard before. Leaves one hell of a mental image."

I nodded since I'd experienced the same.

"But," Ernie continued, "it's utter malarkey. There hasn't been a robbery attempt at the bank in better than thirty years."

Since Vernon had brought up the subject, I asked, "Do you know if Jober had family in the area?"

A frown marred Ernie's forehead as he shook his head. "Not here, no. I was able to locate his sister. She's in Ohio, and before you ask, she has no idea who would have wanted to kill him. They hadn't spoken since he moved to Mooselick River. By his choice, she said."

"That's too bad. From what Vernon told me, Jober lost his wife and kids in a house fire." I didn't have to ask if the information tracked with what Ernie might have learned because he was already nodding.

"Tragic accident. Cumberland County sheriff's office sent me a copy of the reports. The fire marshal ruled out arson, but Jober refused to accept the truth."

"Do you think he was the way he was because of the fire? Like the tall tales are his way of compensating or something. Did you ask his sister?"

Snorting, Ernie said, "And how do you think that conversation would go? Hey, did your brother lie like a bad rug all his life, or was this just a recent phase?"

I rolled my eyes. "You could probably phrase it with a bit more tact, but don't you think it would be helpful to know?"

"Why?"

"I don't know. Isn't it your job to investigate?"

"As opposed to it being yours?"

This wasn't getting me anywhere other than moving me higher on Ernie's naughty list, so I conceded the point and said I'd probably better get to the motel to open for the day. Ernie certainly didn't argue, so we parted ways. On an unsure footing, but what else is new?

CHAPTER TWENTY-SIX

One week after the unfortunate incident, Cappy's reopened with someone new taking Milo's place behind the bar.

"Ghoulish, isn't it?" Neena leaned across the table to be heard over the voices of people jamming every single table. "Nothing like avid curiosity and a former crime scene to pack in a crowd."

Jacy caught my eye and grinned but didn't point out the pot-and-kettle nature of the comment, given we were also there at the time. Instead, she said, "Whatever the reason, I'm glad to see the place didn't go all ghost town. I was worried the owners might decide to shut it down if it didn't open back up soon. I wonder if they'll hire that new guy and let Milo go."

Since it wasn't my secret to tell, I hadn't dropped the Milo-owns-the-bar bomb, but I shook my head. "So long as he's not in jail for a crime he didn't commit, Milo's job is safe. I have it on good authority."

The others might have pressed for more information if Miranda hadn't materialized with a loaded tray of appetizers. Under the guise of setting the food on the table, she leaned in and nodded her head toward the woman serving tables down on the main floor. "Don't everyone look, but that's Milo's wife hustling drinks over there. First time for everything, I suppose."

We looked. Of course, we did. Since I'd never actually met the woman, I wanted to see how she matched up to her phone voice. Her brow, beneath ruler-straight ebony bangs, furrowed as she transferred bottles of beer from tray to table.

"What's her name?" I asked because if I'd ever heard it before, I couldn't dredge up the memory.

"Mina." As expected, Jacy knew, but her brows shot up when Mina turned. "That's new."

"What?" Neena leaned sideways to get a better look.

"If I'm not mistaken, Mina's got a baby bump. I didn't know they were expecting." Unconsciously, Jacy moved her hand to her own belly. When she noticed me noticing, she shook her head slightly. Not yet.

"One more reason to figure out what happened here the other night," Patrea said once Miranda had gone. "Speaking of which, I met with Jenny Sandler this afternoon."

We all stopped to watch as Jacy squirted ketchup, mustard, and tartar on a small plate, spun a knife through to swirl them together. She tested the mixture with a fried green bean, then grabbed a packet of lemon juice from the bowl in the center of the table, added that to the rest, and tested again. Since it was there, she dashed in some

Parmesan from the shaker, but when she picked up the bottle of malt vinegar, Neena let out a disgusted sound.

"What?" Jacy shot up a brow, tipped the bottle, shook the tart, dark liquid over the rest, and went for the steak sauce next.

"That's just nasty." Neena stuck with straight ketchup, went for a golden nugget of fried cauliflower, and used it to gesture toward Jacy. "Are you sure you're not in the same boat as Mina?"

"Not for lack of trying," Jacy wrinkled her nose. "But no, I'm not. That I know of, anyway."

"So, you're saying there's no excuse for what you just did?"

Jacy shrugged and dipped another bean. "Nope."

"If we could get back to the topic at hand," Patrea held up one of hers to block out the sight of Jacy's plate, "before we got distracted by culinary chaos, I was about to tell you why we can absolutely rule out Jenny Sandler."

"Absolutely?" Neena speared an onion from the bowl of mixed pickles, popped it in her mouth, then waved her fork to indicate Patrea should continue.

"I say *absolutely* because her motive was weak, and she didn't have the means." After draining her wineglass, Patrea leaned forward and rested her elbows on the table. "There's no way Jenny stabbed anyone last Friday night because she'd just had carpal tunnel surgery the Tuesday before."

"On both hands?" Glop dripped from a piece of fried

pickle as Jacy waved her fork around and mimed using it to stab. "Only takes one."

Grinning, Patrea shook her head. "As soon as this one heals, she's having the other one done. She can just about hold a fork with her left hand, and she definitely couldn't have gripped a knife with her right hand that soon after the surgery."

"I guess that's one down, then." I flicked my index finger through the air to mark her off an invisible list. "But I still want to know what he had on her."

"He saw her taking a bribe from a local business owner."

"Really?" Jacy frowned. "Who was it?"

When Patrea merely pointed at her, Jacy frowned again. "Me? But, I didn't...that's...it's," then the light dawned on her. "For crying out loud. That wasn't a bribe. It was payment for a mid-century dresser. She wanted it, then waffled. I ran into her in the grocery store, and she handed me the cash before she could change her mind again."

"A transaction made in a public place where poor Mr. Peavey was doing one of his odd jobs. He saw money exchanging hands, and his imagination went to work."

The conversation paused again while Miranda cleared the table, then delivered the salads we'd all agreed we should order as our main course to counteract the unhealthy appetizers. When she'd gone, Patrea dipped a cherry tomato into the dressing she'd ordered on the side.

"I feel bad for him because I'm not sure he understood the difference between reality and the sordid world he created in his head. Having a suspicious nature shouldn't be grounds for murder."

"Well, I suppose he's in a better place now." Neena's dark eyes radiated sympathy. "He's probably looking down and seeing the good he missed in everyone."

No. He wasn't. He was skulking around town, still thinking I was the spawn of Satan. Somehow, I doubted the rest of the townspeople fared any better in his estimation. Eventually, I'd have to make a point of trying to get through to him, but tonight, the best thing I could do for Jober was to try and figure out who killed him.

"One of his stories must have hit home, or else I can't see much of a motive to kill him," I said. "No one seems to know much about his personal life. I did find out he'd lost his wife and children in a fire. Maybe we're making a mistake following the effects of his tall tales, but this avenue seems right to me."

Because she's made that way, Jacy's eyes clouded with sympathy. "That poor man. He might have been annoying, but he deserves justice."

"We must have missed someone who was there that night." Neena reached for the list, but Jacy snatched it back.

"Maybe." I'd already detailed my conversation with Bennie, but I hadn't said anything about Vernon. Given his family ties to Jacy's husband, I figured the less said about him as a former suspect, the better. "Unless he had a woman no one has heard about."

Miranda checked to see if we needed anything else on her way past our table. When she'd gone, Patrea lifted her newly-filled glass, but before sipping, put it back down. "No one has mentioned anything like that. Do you think it was a woman at all? I mean, it takes some punch to stab a man in the back, right? Seems more like something a guy would do."

"That's sexist," I pointed out.

"Is it?" Patrea shrugged. "I wasn't thinking of it that way."

Neena grinned wickedly. "We are women. We are mighty with knives. Betray us at your own risk."

Something about the conversation touched off a niggling thought that wouldn't come clear. The harder I tried to nail it down, the farther away it seemed to get. Kind of the same way an item on a top cabinet shelf will skitter back from your fingertips. Highly annoying.

When I tuned back in, Neena had moved on to give details of her conversation with Darcy Campbell.

"Two glasses of wine and that woman would tell you where Jimmy Hoffa was buried if she knew. Three and she'd tell you if she was the one who buried him, but it only took one to get her to spill her dirty secret."

She had our attention.

"Do you want the truth first, or Oddjob's version?"

"Truth," I spoke first and cemented the deal.

Neena nodded. "Okay, so Darcy's cousin went through a nasty breakup after a long-term relationship and needed a place to stay. He's been bunking in their spare room for the last two months."

"Aw, that's too bad," Jacy said. "But it's nothing scandalous."

"It is," Neena wagged a finger, "if you have decided that the three of them are now a couple."

"Ew," I said, thinking of my male cousins. Patrea echoed the sentiment.

"Ew, indeed." Neena nodded. "Darcy laughed it off and said if people didn't know her any better than that, they could think whatever they wanted."

Since the Campbells were sitting at their usual Friday night table, we all turned to cast speculative eyes over the couple. "Is anyone else picturing it?"

"Shut up," Jacy grinned. "I was trying not to, and now I can't stop. Quick, talk about something else? Otherwise, I'll be forced to gouge out a chunk of my brain."

"Don't do that," Neena returned the grin. "You might lose the part that can figure out the tax without using a calculator."

Before they got too deep into the teasing, I turned to Neena and said, "Did Darcy point the finger anywhere else? Jober didn't seem to have many friends, and everyone I've talked to has heard a worse story than theirs. It's like a daisy chain of whackadoodle gossip."

Finishing off her salad, Patrea set down her fork. "I

never met the man, but I can't decide if I feel more sorry for him because of how he died or how he lived. You can't be a happy person if you view the entire world as a hotbed of sordid activity."

I couldn't fault Patrea's logic, nor could I tell her Jober's afterlife hadn't changed him much. Of all the ghosts I'd met so far, he and Davina proved the least helpful for different reasons. He thought he was in hell, and she couldn't accept that someone had disliked her enough to want her dead.

"I guess we can cross both of the Campbells off the list." Jacy reached around for her purse and pulled out the little notebook. "Unless you think we still need to talk to Nelson." She cocked her head, looked at Neena, who shook hers.

"Probably not, but you were right. She did mention someone else we should add to the list."

Her pen poised over the paper, Jacy waited. "I'm almost afraid to ask."

"It seems Patricia Croft ran over her neighbor's dog, buried it in her backyard, and told everyone she'd seen it chase a cat into the woods."

I choked on a sip of wine. "You have got to be kidding," I said once Patrea had whacked me on the back, and I got my breath again.

Neena shook her head. "I wish I was, but that's what Darcy said."

"If you'd have said it was Bess Tate, I wouldn't bat an

eyelash, but not Patricia. She sometimes gives off a still-waters vibe, but I just can't see her doing something like that."

"Like what?" Jacy frowned. "Hitting the dog or lying about it?"

I thought for a moment, then had to admit. "No. If she hit the dog and thought she could spare the owner's feelings, she'd lie her ass off right to their faces. But Patricia is the least ambitious person I know when it comes to physical labor. She wouldn't have the gumption to bury anything."

"Gumption," Patrea said. "There's a word you don't hear every day."

"It was one of Grammie Dupree's favorites."

Jacy tapped the pen on the table twice, then crossed Darcy's name off the list. "Obviously, we'll revisit if more information comes to light, but for now, we're down to," she checked over her shoulder just in case, "Miranda on the original list, plus we've ruled out a bunch of people who weren't even on there, to begin with."

"You can cross off Miranda." I waggled a finger at Jacy. "Turns out she moonlights at the Bide-A-Way sometimes, and while I was filling in for Barbara, I got a chance to talk to her and learned her unforgivable sin was watering down the booze."

"The horror." Jacy drew a line through Miranda's name, then almost as an afterthought, she noted the epithets Jober had thrown out on the night of his death, writing cheat next to Bennie's name, adulterer next to Darcy and Nelson's.

"Does that make Miranda the liar or the thief?"

"Dunno," I shrugged. "Could be either, neither, or both, given that none of Jober's ridiculous stories have been true so far. Did I tell you he thought Robin Thackery was in a cult?"

Jacy's eyes went wide, then she snorted. "That's one rumor I have no trouble believing, except I can't imagine a cult that would take her, and I know she's only selling makeup. It's really good makeup, but even so."

Rock music pounded out of the jukebox at a higher than normal level. I had to squint to see who the couple that danced in front of it was.

"Looks like Thea's moved on," I said and pointed. "That's not Jason she's doing the sexy dance with. It's Martin Walker from the bank."

Neena took one look at the gyrating couple and shuddered. "I think I just threw up in my mouth."

"Is Jason here?" Jacy tilted her head and spotted him at the table where he'd been sitting the week before. When Miranda passed by, Jacy grabbed her and paid to have a drink sent to Jason. "Tell him he'd better be here celebrating his near miss, and I don't want to catch him crying in his beer."

CHAPTER TWENTY-SEVEN

"I should have gone with red instead of white wine." Drew brandished the bottle he carried as we walked up the drive toward my parent's front porch on Wednesday night. It was his first family dinner there since we'd moved in together, and I found his display of nerves slightly amusing.

"White's fine." I put a hand on his arm. "Relax. My mother loves you."

"She's not the one who worries me. Your dad tossed some pretty broad hints about my intentions the last time we had dinner."

"Leave him to me."

"Or you could just say yes. You know, just to get him off my back."

Stopping him, I made deliberate eye contact. "When I decide to marry you, it won't have anything to do with my father, okay?"

"You said when, not if," he pointed out.

"Maybe I did."

Of course, I'd been thinking about our future, and for Drew, that meant marriage and babies, and no matter how much I tried to convince myself I didn't, I wanted those things, too. But once bitten, twice shy. "Try not to let it go to your head."

He leaned down and kissed me on the end of the nose. "You go to my head just like this fine wine. I can't promise I won't ask again."

I'd probably say yes if he did, but he didn't need to know that right now. I'd rather hold out until Davina left the building and took my ability to see ghosts with her.

"It's okay. I can't promise my dad won't bring it up again. If he does, you can distract him with questions about power tools."

"Noted."

Old Blue barked up a storm as we stepped onto the porch of the slate-gray craftsman-style house decorated for fall. Burgundy mums and pumpkins in orange and white spilled from pedestals made of logs with the bark still on. Sprays of silk foliage in yellows, reds, and orange speared from galvanized pails to lend height to the arrangement.

As it always did when I walked into my childhood home, my gaze tracked to the touchstones of familiarity: photos on the mantel, mother's snow globes, a few of Grammie Dupree's bells, and the hundreds of books lining the built-in shelves.

Next to me, Drew sighed, and I swiveled my head to see why. "You okay?"

"Sure. I just love this house. It's such a blend of your folks. It's perfect."

He was right, and I loved him even more for noticing the woodwork my dad had meticulously stripped back after a former owner had the temerity to paint it white. The saturated paint colors and variety of patterns on pillows and throws were all my mom's doing.

The contrast between him and my ex-husband hit me as I leaned down to give the dog some love. Yeah, if he asked, the answer would be yes. No probably about it.

"We're in the kitchen," my mom called out as I hung our coats. "Come on back."

I took two steps before I realized Drew wasn't following. He stood near the fireplace, looking at a photo of Jacy and me standing on the end of the dock at her parent's camp.

"Do you remember this?"

"Not really. I spent a lot of time on the lake with the Wades." But it was the year Jacy had taken the scissors to her hair and ended up with a somewhat ragged pixie cut. "Why?"

He pointed to one of the kids swimming in the background

"That's me. This must have been the year we first met."

"Really?" I looked closer and tapped my finger against the glass. "You were watching us."

"Couldn't help myself. Look at the pair of you, like fire and ice."

All I saw was a round-faced girl with a tumble of unruly red curls and freckles. Calling me fire seemed a bit of an exaggeration, but he wasn't wrong about Jacy. With her blue eyes and hair bleached almost white by the sun, she could have been cast in the role of ice princess.

I put the photo back where it belonged.

"I remember that exact moment," Drew said, his smile nostalgic. "It was the hottest day of the summer, and Jacy refused to get in the water because she was waiting for you. Then this car pulls in, and this barefoot bundle of fire races toward the dock."

He could have been describing any day at Jacy's camp, but he wasn't. This was a special day to him, and I wished I remembered it better.

"Then Mrs. Wade yelled for you to stop and came out with the camera, so you waited for her."

The memory niggled loose. "She took forever to line up the shot."

He nodded. "When she was done, the two of you walked it way back, did a high-five, and—"

"Did our famous running handsprings with a double somersault off the end of the dock."

"You remember."

I did. "We were nine and had just finished a summer session of tumbling classes, so we were showing off."

"Well, it was a sight that left a lasting impression on me. You took my breath away. You still do."

"You two get lost or something?" My dad called from the kitchen.

Grinning, I offered Drew a quick kiss. "From the smell of it, Dad's making his famous chili. Be warned, I'm not the only one in the family that can take your breath away." Taking his hand, I pulled him toward the spicy scents and warmth of the heart of my childhood home.

"Something sure smells good." Drew earned points with the compliment and more by asking if there was anything he could do to help.

"Under control." Dad wore a kiss the cook apron, so I walked over to give him a hug and a kiss on the cheek. In return, he dipped a wooden spoon into the bubbling contents of the pot, blew on it to cool, and held it for me to taste. "I think it's my best batch ever."

I tasted spice and heat balanced with just the right amount of sweetness to keep it from being too savory and something new—something familiar but different. I closed my eyes to figure it out. "Did you use maple syrup?"

"I did."

My mother stepped up for her hug and kiss on the cheek. "Someone," and the look she tossed at my dad gave him no room to deny, "has been putting honey in their coffee."

"You told me I had to cut back on sugar." But he could defend.

"Since we were almost out, I made cornbread with most of it, so he had to compromise."

"Sometimes," my dad said. "Our greatest strokes of genius are a result of overcoming adversity."

My mother did not find his observation profound. "What you need to overcome is your sugar addiction."

"Yes, dear."

"Anyway," Kitty Dupree ignored her husband's attempt to placate her. "I spoke to Barb Dexter yesterday. She said to tell you she has pictures of the baby if you want to stop in sometime."

"I'll do that. I'm glad she made it in time to attend the birth."

She handed me a basket of cornbread to carry while my dad poured chili into a large tureen. "She almost didn't. They hit some headwinds on the trip out, and only made it to the hospital with two hours to spare. The baby came a day or two earlier than expected."

Then, proving my dad wasn't the only one who could put pressure on my love life, she said, "I'm glad I'll have the luxury of being there for every stage when it's my time for grandchildren." With barely a pause, she pinned me with a look. "And when will that be?"

The basket of bread bobbled as I set it on the table.

"Um." My tongue went thick. "Did dad put you up to that?" I glanced over to see him putting on his innocent face, but I had my doubts.

"Give me time," Drew grinned and changed the

subject while we all settled around the table. "Would you mind if I borrowed the photo of Everly and Jacy from your mantel? I'd like to get a copy made."

"If you like." My mother added cheese to her chili. "Do you mind me asking why that particular photo?"

"Not at all." Drew shook his head. "If you look closely, you'll see two boys swimming in the background. One of them is Jacy's brother. The other is me, and the picture was taken on the day Everly and I first met."

You wouldn't know it on first meeting her, but the path to my mother's heart is paved with sentimental stones. If he hadn't already charmed her, he did now. My dad, of course, used the chance to push the marriage angle because he was even more of a marshmallow than my mom. I managed to change the subject and start my fishing expedition by mentioning my trip to the bank.

"I didn't know Mr. Herbert had retired."

"Is that how they put it?" Annoyed, my dad stabbed his knife into the butter, cut off more than he needed, and said a few words he rarely used.

You can tell when my dad's blood pressure goes up because his hair goes puffy. We joke about it, but we also use it as a barometer for his mood. Talking about his friend pushed the hair to level seven, which wasn't good.

"I take it he wasn't planning to retire. Did it have to do with rumors of a robbery attempt?"

Oops, make that a level eight.

"Where did you get that idea?" My mother frowned at

me, then laid her hand on my dad's arm to help calm him down. "Harold Herbert is as honest as anyone you'll ever meet."

"I'm sorry, dad. I didn't mean to cast aspersions on your friend. I was just repeating something Jober had been saying."

"Ah, well then." We were back to a level five and trending lower. "Jober was known for getting things wrong."

The tingle that set goosebumps prickling across my skin had nothing to do with ghosts, but the chill that wafted across the back of my neck did. I flicked a glance at my mother, who stared at whoever was behind me—presumably Davina since Jober wouldn't come near me. When Mom lifted a brow, then looked at me with dismay, I turned to see it was both, and Jober wasn't looking too good.

Horrible timing.

"Isn't this nice," Davina's proximity sent another chill down my neck. "Having dinner with the family while poor Jober is stuck on the wrong side of the veil."

Tension gathered at my temples, setting them to a slow throb while I searched for something to say that wouldn't sound batcrap crazy to my dad or Drew. The only thing that came to mind wasn't especially flattering to Jober, but I felt like I was on the edge of learning something important.

"I've spent over a week trying to find the nuggets of

truth in the more salacious of Jober's tall tales because I think one of his stories got him killed. Maybe if he hadn't told so many of them, I'd be done already."

Because she'd circled around to where she could see my face, I got a good look at Davina's too. The squint of her eyes read as annoyance, but the tightness on the sides of her mouth said something else. If I wasn't mistaken, Davina was afraid. Not, I sensed, of Jober, but of what might happen to him if I didn't sort this mystery out soon.

My mother stared at him in horror, but I didn't dare turn around for a closer look with my dad sitting right there. Not that my mother's expression wouldn't require some explanation if she didn't get control of it and fast. I kicked her under the table, but it was too late.

"Something wrong, dear?" Dad tilted his head and assessed. "You look like you've seen a ghost."

The deadpan tone gave him away.

"You know, don't you? You've known all along." The second the words left my lips, I regretted them. I'd just made amends with my mother and didn't need something else to set off another disagreement.

"Known what? That your mother has the ghost vision? I'd have to be blind and stupid to miss the clues. I'm neither. You have it, too."

Color rushed into my mother's face. "You never said a word. How long have you known?"

If only the floor would open up and swallow me whole. Under the table, Drew took my hand, squeezed gently to give what comfort he could. I squeezed back because this was not the time to apologize for dropping him into the middle of a family fracas.

"You do remember who raised me, right?"

If you put my straitlaced mother on one end of the woo-woo scale and plopped Leandra Wade on the other, my grandmother would have fallen somewhere in the middle. Grammie Dupree had the sight but, unlike Leandra, had sense enough not to dabble in things she couldn't fully control. And yes, I might still be bitter that Leandra's meddling opened me to my own latent abilities. No offense to Grammie Dupree, but I was fine to have her eyes and wild, red hair and could have done without inheriting anything else. Not that I did, I supposed, since I couldn't see the future. Nope, it was all my mother's fault.

"I feel...well, I don't know how I feel," my mother pressed a shaking hand to her brow. "It's not like I see ghosts every day or anything. It's only happened a few times."

"I'd hoped you'd tell me if my mother came to you." My father chose his words carefully, so they were both statement and question delivered without any sense of condemnation. He really was the best person I knew.

My mother sucked in a breath, and her mouth worked, but nothing came out, so she merely shook her head and then put one hand over her eyes, the other over her heart.

"Kitty." Dad rose, rounded the table to pull her up and

into a hug. "It's okay. You don't have to talk about it if you aren't ready."

I'd honestly forgotten Davina and Jober were there until Davina dripped sarcasm all over the room. "If you're done with your little family confessional, we have an actual crisis on our hands."

Dad's head came up, his arms going tight enough that my mother squirmed in his embrace.

Drew twitched like he did whenever Davina showed herself, which I regretted telling her how to do.

"Good," Davina continued. "It looks like everyone's finally listening." Beside her, Jober stared at the floor, his mouth working but no sound coming out. Maybe Davina had hit some sort of ghostly mute button on him.

Maybe I could get her to tell me how that worked.

"What can we do to help?" You had to give my dad credit for a fast recovery and more credit for wanting to help when he had to be reeling from the weirdness of the moment.

"This is not my area of expertise," Davina waved a hand toward Jober, who stood, head down, muttering to himself. "But I think if he keeps channeling his energy into denying his new reality, he might not be able to cross over. So stop playing around, and figure out who killed him."

The temperature in the room took a nosedive.

"I'm doing the best I can, but he had something nasty

to say about nearly everyone in town, so the suspect pool is more like a lake."

While we bickered, my mother stood and circled the table.

"Jober," she spoke gently, reached out as if to touch his arm, then let her hand drop. "It's Kitty Dupree. Do you remember me?"

Still muttering, he nodded but didn't look up.

"I'd like to help you if you'll let me. Please."

None of us were prepared for the sight when Jober finally lifted his head and glared with eyes red and glowing as a hot ember. And he'd thought I was the spawn of Satan.

Drew's chair scraped across the floor as he left it to put the table between him and Jober. "What the hell?"

"Now, do you see what I've been dealing with?" The temperature dropped a few more degrees when Davina spoke, but I barely noticed the cold because I was too busy trying to shake off a case of the heebie-jeebies. "It's bad, right?"

"It is, but I know someone who knows more about this stuff than I do. If we haven't sorted him out within the next couple of days, I'll make a call and see what she has to say." It was the best I could offer. "But I feel like we're close to a breakthrough." Or I had a few minutes ago, and now, I couldn't remember why.

"Fine." Davina tossed her head. "I'll just let you get back to your cozy little dinner party." But for spite, she locked eyes with me while she poked her finger into the tureen of chili, which froze solid, then she grabbed Jober by the arm and faded them both away.

Dead silence followed her exit until Drew finally spoke up. "Well, that was fun."

A rush of activity followed Davina's exit. My father went back to the kitchen, returned with the pot containing what was left of the chili. "This is still warm if anyone's still hungry."

"How can you think of food at a time like this?" Still flushed, my mother emptied her wineglass, poured more, and drained that as well.

Dad shrugged and topped off his bowl. "We'll all think better with full stomachs. Now, Everly, you'd better tell us what you know."

And so, while my mother sipped her third glass of wine, I laid it all out for them. By the time I'd come to the story about Mr. Herbert, we'd all finished our interrupted meal. Even my mom had cleaned her bowl.

"Somebody got their wires crossed on that one," Dad said. "Harry was up for a promotion to branch manager, and he'd been promised the job, but when the time came, they "decided to go another way"." He did air quotes. "Which means Harry got passed over. They gave the job to some young fellow from one another branch."

"I met him. His name's Martin Walker, and he's not very discreet." After his gaffe at the dealership, I'd begun to regret transferring my money to the local bank. But anyway, Davina kind of rained on my parade. Drew knew what I meant, but my parents looked mystified. Of course, my dad jumped to his most hoped-for conclusion.

"You're engaged?"

For the joy in his face alone, I might have wished the answer was yes, but it wasn't, so I shook my head and hoped the actual surprise would take away some of the sting. "Not yet. But I do have a surprise for you." Reaching into my pocket, I pulled out my—about to be his—car keys and dangled them over the table.

My mom caught on immediately, and I gave her a wink, but my dad merely frowned, so I shook the keys at him. "These are for you."

He still didn't get it.

"You'll need them if you want to drive your new car."

The light began to dawn, but only enough to see a glimmer of daylight. "You're not giving me your car." He shook his head.

"Oh, but I am. You love her more than I do, and besides, I've totally cheated on Sally. Come outside and see."

He still wouldn't take the keys, but he did stand to follow me out. When my mother moved to rise, Drew caught her eye, shook his head, and she settled back down. "You go," she waved a hand. "It's cold out."

As we left the room, I heard her whisper something to Drew.

"Grab a coat," I said when my dad would have gone out without one. "Mom's right about the cold."

Outside, I introduced him to my new ride. "I figured the all-wheel drive is more practical for winter roads. Even in red, this one's not nearly as flashy as Sally, but I don't need two vehicles." I held out the keys. "So I was hoping you'd take good care of her from here on out."

This time, he took them.

"Are you sure?"

I hugged him. "I am. Drew got her all polished up for you, and Bennie gave her the once-over, so she's had his stamp of approval. Call it an early Christmas present if you must, but she's all yours. I think Catherine would approve."

"I'm more worried about what your mother will say." He pulled me in for the best dad hug ever. "But she'll just have to deal with it. Thanks, honey. I'll drive her with pride."

And that was why Bennie never stood a chance. Sally was meant for my dad. They belonged together.

CHAPTER TWENTY-EIGHT

"That went well," I said with no trace of sarcasm at all when we were driving home. "I thought my dad might be upset that I didn't ask him to go car shopping with me."

Drew laughed. "I think you did a fine job of distracting him." He reached over, took my hand. "His feet were barely touching the floor the rest of the night. I like your family, by the way. They'll make great in-laws when you finally get around to marrying me."

"Someone's getting cocky." I couldn't help but smile.

"Well, you did say when, not if."

"How about you let me get Jober and Davina safely sorted, and then we'll talk about it again?"

He patted my leg, then put his hand back on the steering wheel to make the turn at the end of the street. "Count on it. What can I do? I have a vested interest in helping them now."

"Fine. We'll stick with Jober for now since I have no suspects for Davina and half a town's worth for him. Did you pick up on anything when I explained it all to my folks?"

We spent the rest of the drive home rehashing the details, and even though we didn't come up with anything new, my head felt clearer than it had in days.

"My current theory is that one of his stories had more truth than embellishment, and someone needed to shut him up."

By then, we were snuggled on the sofa with Molly at our feet.

"What about Jober's wife's family? Could be someone wanted revenge for her death."

"But why now? It seems like a long time to wait."

Drew shrugged. "Maybe. Unless Jober didn't keep in touch when he moved and they lost track of him, or else they were smart enough to wait until her death wouldn't seem like a good motive. How long ago was the fire?"

Good question.

"You know, I'm not sure." Rising, I stepped over the dog and went to get my laptop. "But I bet I can find out. Everything's online these days, and a tragedy like that tends to end up in the news."

Thanks to my mother forcing me to learn how to use the archive function on the library website, it didn't take long to find the news report or to realize I should have looked before. Drew leaned in and read the tragic story along with me.

"No wonder Jober was so messed up. He couldn't accept that the fire was an accident, and I think he probably suffered from survivor's guilt on top of everything else. I feel sorry for him. I get why people were annoyed with the things he said, and without context, I'm sure I'd have felt the same."

His voice quiet, Drew said, "People carry their emotional scars under the skin. Makes it hard to know how deep the cuts were or how well they've healed."

"If I can help him move on, I hope he'll be reunited with his family on the other side. It's all I can do for him now." To further that goal, I finished reading the article. When I was done, I accidentally bumped the arrow button that scrolled through previous articles and was just about to close the browser window when a headline caught my attention.

"Bank Robbery Foiled by Teller," I read out loud, then looked at the date. "I bet this is where Jober came up with the idea that Mr. Herbert had something to do with a bank robbery. It happened just a few days before the fire and probably stuck in his head."

Because it was right in front of me, I began to read the article. "Whoa," I said when I read the teller's name. "That's Martin Walker. He lived right near Jober and supposedly foiled a bank robbery, and now, he's here in Mooselick River, too."

A rush of energy went through me. So much that I needed to get some of it out. Hastily, I shoved the laptop onto Drew's lap and began to pace.

"There has to be a connection. Otherwise, there's just too much coincidence for me to swallow."

Meanwhile, Drew ran a new search for information on Martin Walker. "It says here that he was helping a customer when he heard noises in the wall behind the vault and took steps to stop the robbery almost before it began."

"You sound skeptical," I said because he did, and considering I felt the same but couldn't put my finger on the reason, asked, "Why?"

Taking a moment to frame his thoughts, his brow furrowed, Drew finally set the laptop down on the coffee table, then shook his head. "I don't know. What was Jober's bank robbery story?"

"I don't have a lot of details. All I know is that Vernon told me that Jober told him that Mr. Herbert master-minded an attempt to rob the bank." The niggling thought in the back of my head came clear. "But what if it wasn't Mr. Herbert at all? What if Jober was talking about Martin Walker instead?"

I was onto something. I felt it in my bones.

Until Drew pointed out the flaw in my theory. "Doesn't make sense. Why would Walker plan a heist and then turn around and foil the attempt?"

Deflated, I flopped back down next to him. "I have no idea. Was anyone arrested?" Since my laptop had gone to sleep, I tapped a key to wake it back up but Drew filled in the blanks before the screen flared back to life.

"Nope. Long gone by the time the cops arrived. As far as I could see, the case remains open and unsolved, but Martin Walker's quick thinking earned him a promotion—in a smaller bank."

"And that's how he ended up in Mooselick River at the same bar where Jober started throwing around a bunch of wild accusations, only this was the one time he got it right. Or at least mostly right."

Drew nodded. "Let's say you're right. What do we do about it?"

"No idea. I don't have enough evidence to take to Ernie, and he's not too happy with me right now, anyway, so even if I did, he might blow me off out of spite. Walker has no idea we're looking at him, and I bet he's feeling pretty safe with Jober out of the way."

For a moment, Drew remained silent, then he said, "I think that's a fair assessment, so since we have a minute, I say we rally the troops and form a plan of attack." If the light in his eyes was anything to go by, he would enjoy this. "I'd like to have one of these murders solved where you don't end up bruised or battered at the end of it."

Hey, I hadn't healed from the last go around, so I wasn't about to argue with his logic. "It's nice to know you have my back."

"Always," he said as he leaned over to gather me in for a kiss. "And forever."

When he let me go again, I began to type in the group text we used for planning game nights:

Dinner at my place tomorrow night. We'll do Mexican and plan how to catch a killer. You in?

After a moment's thought, I backspaced and changed *my place* to *our place.*

CHAPTER TWENTY-NINE

"What if he doesn't show up?" Neena asked for the second time as we pulled into the space next to Chris Evergreen's truck in the parking lot at Cappy's on Friday night.

"He's already returned to the scene once, and I have no doubt he'll do it again. He has no idea we're onto him, so if he doesn't show tomorrow night, we can wait until he does," Drew patiently explained.

But her part of the setup was the most precarious, so I understood her trepidation.

"The only thing that would make this mission cooler is if we had those little earpieces for communication." I'd figured David for possibly being a hold-out, but he'd surprised me by getting totally into the plan. "But you don't have to worry, Neena, we've got you."

Jacy and Brian had pulled in right behind us, and we all took a moment for last-minute checks before going inside.

"You spoke to Milo?" I asked her, and Jacy nodded.

"He's totally on board, and thrilled to have a part in catching Jober's killer. Not that he didn't trust Ernie to get to the bottom of things eventually, but sooner is better than later, so Milo's ready to go."

Jacy ticked off the points she'd been told to pass along. "The clothes he was wearing that night will be in a bag under the seat of our usual table, which Miranda's keeping an eye on so no one takes. We went over the timing, so they're both up to date and ready. Looks like Ernie took the bait." She pointed to the truck the cop drove when he was off-duty.

"All we need now is for the banker to show up. Do you think he will?" Neena sounded less anxious and more eager than before.

"Even if he doesn't, we have time," I said. "Walker has no idea we're onto him."

"If things go south tonight, we'll have to come up with another reason to get Ernie here in plain clothes next week, but I have a feeling that won't be the case. Thea's already here, and she told Mabel she only needed one more shot at it to—as she put it—bag the banker."

"Okay, good. You're wearing the right boots, Chris?" I checked his feet, but it was too dark to tell.

"Got them. Show me the photo one more time, though. Just so I have it in my head."

I pulled out my phone and scrolled to the photo of Jober's body. Let Chris take a long look.

"I'm good. We all in?" He put his hand out in front of him.

"Bet your ass," Patrea's hand slapped onto her

husband's. "Whoever said small towns were boring never came to Mooselick River. I haven't had a dull moment since I came here."

One by one, four more hands joined the pile.

"Let's do this." Breaking formation, we all turned to head inside. This time, it felt more like a wind in the hair moment.

"He's here." The first inside, Neena laid eyes on Martin Walker and passed the word back to the rest of us.

Jacy split off and headed toward the bar to speak with Milo while the rest of us crowded around our usual table. When she returned, she gave the thumbs up. "We're good to go. Ernie showed up right before we did, so we have a little time. Let the man at least eat his Cappy Burger before we interrupt his meal."

We hadn't even ordered when Miranda showed up with a tray of appetizers for the table. "On the house. Compliments of Milo for all your help, and I'll be right back with drinks." She took our order leaving me to wonder how much he'd told her. Not that it mattered now.

Too keyed up by our mission, we picked at the food while we watched for the right time to deploy.

"Okay," Neena said after ten minutes or so. "They're up and dancing the dance of imminent sexy times. We'd better get moving before they take it outside or something." Her color was high because the beginning of the plan rested on her. Well, on her and David.

The two joined Thea and Martin Walker on the dance floor for one song, then another, while Brian circled around to the shadows behind the jukebox. Drew and I headed for the bar, and when the second song ended, Brian yanked the power plug to stop the music, which was my cue.

Drew lifted me like I weighed nothing and helped me to stand on the bar. "Hey, everyone!" I yelled. "Let's all raise a glass to celebrate Milo's return to Cappy's. Long may he pour the best drinks in town."

"It's the only drinks in town," someone yelled back, and most of the crowd cheered, but the point was, everyone—including Martin Walker—paid attention to Milo when he stood to offer a speech of heartfelt thanks.

When Drew helped me down, I spoke in his ear. "That's phase one. Now, it's Neena's turn."

As soon as Milo finished speaking, Brian plugged the jukebox back in, and from my spot near the bar, I caught Patrea's eye and nodded. She and Chris rose and began to make their way toward the kitchen door while Jacy went the other way to drop coins in the jukebox and pick the two songs we'd chosen in advance.

From my vantage point on the platform near the bar, I saw Patrea and Chris slide into the kitchen, watched Milo have a word with the new bartender before he followed. Everything was working just like we planned.

I should have known it was all too easy.

"What's going on?" A chill shivered up my neck when Davina popped up next to me.

"Nothing. Go away."

She, of course, didn't go away and merely repeated, "What's going on?"

"Look, stay or go. I don't care so long as you keep out of my way. We're here to catch Jober's killer, and I don't need you being a distraction."

A wicked glint came into her eye. "I'll stay. This should be fun to watch."

I shrugged. So long as she didn't do anything distracting, I didn't care what she did.

The first song, a fast number, ended with Neena and David having switched partners with Martin and Thea. Coming back from the kitchen area, Miranda winked at me.

It was go time, and this was the crucial moment in the plan. Neena vamped a bit. Tossed her hair back and gave the banker a good shot of her cleavage while the next song —slow this time—began to play.

David had moves, I'd tease him about that forever, and slid Thea into the slow dance before she knew what hit her, leaving Neena to do the same with Martin.

As he spun her slowly in place, she had to brush his hand off her backside twice. When she caught my eye, her expression spoke of thunder. But all the players were nearly in place. Jacy approached Ernie's table, leaned down to speak to him, then gave me the nod I passed on to Neena, and we hit phase two of the plan.

"Come on," I said to Drew. We split off, heading toward our next positions as nonchalantly as we could while Ernie followed Jacy out the front door. We needed just another minute of leeway to allow her time to lead him around back and get him safely hidden behind the boxes Milo had set up in the storage room.

By then, David had done his part and smoothly maneuvered Thea to the opposite side of the dance floor, using his body to block Martin from her line of sight. If she'd been anyone else, we might have pulled her into the plan, but none of us trusted Thea to a) remember there was a plan and b) do her part to carry it out.

Sagging a bit, Neena let her head fall on Martin's shoulder. I saw him dip his head to speak to her. She let her knees buckle a bit more, and he had no choice but to support her and lead her from the dance floor.

Brian should already be in place at the rear exit in case Walker tried to make a break for it. Drew would move in behind us to guard the kitchen door exit, so the next bit was up to me.

"Is she okay?" I called on my high school play experience and acted concerned. "She doesn't look too good."

Taking her cue, Neena stumbled, forcing him to take more of her weight. "I need someplace quiet to clear my head. Just for a minute."

"Follow me," I said to Walker. "We'll take her through

the kitchen. There's an office on the right. It'll be a good place to sit and get her bearings."

"Office?" Walker frowned. "On the right?"

Yeah. The office was on the left, and because he knew that, he failed the test. But it didn't matter now, we had him in the pipeline, and it was too late for him to escape. At least I wouldn't have to eat crow in front of Ernie. Or not unless our gambit failed and we couldn't get him to admit what he'd done. This part of the operation depended entirely on the element of surprise loosening his tongue.

Everything depended on the next few minutes going well.

"Milo," I called out as I led the way toward the kitchen. "Is it okay if we let Neena sit in the office for a few minutes?"

He waved us on.

"This way," I walked ahead and opened the door to the storage room. Walker balked, but only a little as I pushed the door open, then stepped back as if to get out of his way. When he would have turned around, Neena moaned and sagged a little harder, leaving him no choice but to hold her up and keep going.

"This isn't—" Walker stopped talking when he saw Milo's prone form on the floor and Jober's legs sticking out from between the shelves. Okay, technically, he saw Patrea lying face down dressed as Milo, and the legs belonged to Chris, but the banker saw what we intended for him to see.

I closed the door behind me and walked past the sprawled bodies as if I didn't see them. "There's a chair right here by the desk. Go ahead and help her sit down."

"Are you high?"

No, I wasn't, but Martin Walker's voice certainly was as he stood, his attention riveted on the two X marks scrawled in fresh blood on a crate of Johnnie Walker scotch.

It's not easy to stay quiet sometimes, especially when accusations wanted to fly out of my mouth, but my days of fund-raising had taught me that many people are compelled to speak when silence goes on too long. Martin Walker fell into that category like it was made for him.

"This isn't an office. There are no chairs." He barely noticed when Neena disentangled herself and stepped away from him.

"Then what do you call that?" I presented a confused frown and pointed right at fake Jober's body. "Maybe you're the one who's high."

"Lady, I don't know what game you're playing, but this is a storage room."

From the sudden chill at my back, I knew we had a ghostly audience, but I didn't dare break character. So long as Davina didn't decide to show herself to the world at large, there was probably no reason to worry. And even if there was, it was too late to do anything about it now.

"Maybe you're the one who should sit down. Can I get you some water? You look like you've seen a ghost."

His face perfectly devoid of color, Martin Walker looked from fake Milo to fake Jober and back again. All I needed to do was get him to say something Ernie could use to make a case against him. We'd planned everything to get us to this moment, and I knew I couldn't say anything that would be construed as leading the witness.

Or maybe that was only true on TV. It didn't matter either way because my mind had gone mostly blank except for the mental image of Jober's killer walking away from our only chance to make him pay.

"You're crazy. I'm out of here."

Neena nudged me with her elbow. "Do something," she muttered.

I opened my mouth to say something but never got the chance because the room went cold. Ice cold and clammy. Uh oh.

Jober shivered into visibility and let out a moaning howl that raised the hairs on my neck. Neena stumbled backward and would have fallen on Patrea if I hadn't grabbed her in time.

Behind Jober, Davina sort of knelt with her hands on his back as if she were using him as a shield. The energy level in the storage room spiked until it almost hurt. Patrea jolted, and so did Chris, but Walker didn't notice because Jober's ghost had his full attention.

"Martin Walker," Davina spoke for Jober, lowering her

voice to sound more like him. She lifted his arm to get him to point toward where Chris lay. "Behold the consequences of your actions."

That did not sound like something Jober would say. But I got it now. he wasn't Davina's shield. He was her puppet. Because I could see her anyway, I wasn't sure if everyone else could. Her energy was stronger than most, and she'd been stuck between planes long enough to figure out how things worked. But this was not the time to ask.

Neena sagged against me, this time for real. I had to put some weight behind it to hold her up. "His eyes," she whispered, horrified. "They're red." As if that was the only thing about seeing a ghost that freaked her out. Funnily enough, her horror worked in our favor.

Walker backed away from the ghost only to stumble over Chris, and bless him, Chris never missed a beat.

"Confess your sins, Martin Walker, or burn in hell." He did a better job of nailing the ghost's personality than Davina had.

Not to be outdone, Patrea intoned, "My blood is on your hands."

Walker held his up to check them. They were definitely getting to him.

Eyes alight with unholy glee, Davina shoved Jober forward, "Confess, Martin Walker. Or I will surely haunt you all your days. Confess, or nothing will ever save your mortal soul."

The cheese factor was high, but it didn't matter because she let Jober go and poked Walker in the chest with each word. I almost felt sorry for him because ghost touches rate at least a ten on the heebie jeebie scale.

Walker jolted each time and finally couldn't hold back the truth. "I did it, okay. I hit Milo Lynch in the head with a rolling pin to get him out of the way. Then, I killed Jober Peavey because he found out I'd planned a bank robbery, and he was going to tell my boss. There, I confessed. Big deal. It's your word against mine."

And yet, Martin bolted. He got past me and made it out the door before running smack into Drew. If you've ever seen someone walk into a glass door, you'll have some idea how it looked when Walker's head bounced off Drew's broad chest not once, but twice.

"That's not entirely true."

As Ernie stepped around the corner of the stack of boxes, I shot Davina a pleading look, which she interpreted correctly, and, taking Jober with her, phased out before Ernie locked eyes on the pair of them. A small mercy, to be sure, but at least I'd only have to explain her presence to Neena, Chris, and Patrea. Oh, and David, too. Otherwise, he'd be the only one still in the dark.

"I take it back," Walker tried, but it was a bit too late. "This is entrapment, and that's illegal."

Grunting in disgust, Ernie took a firmer grip on the banker's arm with one hand, pulled out his keys with the other, and tossed them to David, who'd just come in through the back door.

"Looks like I missed all the fun," he said as he caught the keys.

"You know what plastic restraints look like?" Ernie spoke to David, who nodded. "There's a set under the seat of my truck."

Still grinning, David left to retrieve them while Jacy popped out from behind the boxes. "Found it." She winked at Ernie and held up an earring. "Thanks for your help, Officer Polk. Isn't it a lovely coincidence that you were helping me look for my lost earring just as this man confessed to murder?"

David returned quite quickly, handed the restraints over, then took his place next to Neena. "You okay," he asked when he saw her pale face. She wasted no time getting as far away from me as she could.

Given the look on Neena's face as Ernie hauled the banker out the back door of the bar, my confession wouldn't be any easier than his had been. I put it off as long as I could, but before we headed back into the bar proper, I figured it was time to get everything out in the open.

"So I guess some of you have questions, and I'm happy to answer them, but first, I'll just acknowledge the elephant in the room. Yes, I can see ghosts, and no, Davina and Jober weren't my first."

"I knew it," Patrea slugged me on the shoulder. "I told

you your house was haunted at Christmas, and you shrugged it off, but I knew I was right."

"Technically," I qualified, "the house isn't haunted. I am."

Mystified, David frowned. "I couldn't hear much of what was going on, so I think I missed something big."

With exceptional timing, Davina blinked into view.

"What the hell?" David took a step back.

The ghost waved her hand at him dismissively. "Everly sees ghosts, I helped get a confession out of the jerk who killed Jober, and now, we have to get him to cross over. Consider yourself caught up." She turned to me, "Can we please get on with it before it's too late?"

When David's eyes turned toward me, I merely shrugged and shook my head.

"Okay," I said to her. "But this type of thing has never happened to me before. The way it works is that the ghost moves on as soon as the killer is caught. I don't normally have much say in the matter, so I'm not sure what you expect me to do. Are you sure he's still here?"

Davina's thousand-yard stare came with a head-tilt and a side of the shivers, and not just for me because frost began to form on the containers of condiments.

"Knock it off, Davina. I didn't say I wouldn't help Jober. Just tell me what I need to do."

Her retort came quickly. "How the hell should I know?"

"Do you want me to call Momma Wade?" Jacy offered.

"No!" Davina and I answered at the same time. "I'll bring him back so you can talk some sense into him." She blinked out and then back in before anyone else had a chance to say anything.

Red-eyed and slack-jawed, Jober looked worse than ever, but the unearthly light illuminating half of his face made me feel much better.

"Jober," I stepped in front of him and leaned down until we were eye-to-eye. "Jober, can you hear me? I need you to understand that it's okay to go into the light, and I think your family will be there waiting for you. Don't you want to see your family?"

Nothing.

I snapped my fingers in front of his face. He swayed, then, with snake-like speed, jabbed his hand into my throat. I tried to yank my head back but couldn't. And I couldn't breathe around the intense chill, either. My throat felt like a block of ice, and my body shook like a leaf in a gale wind.

"Everly!" I heard Drew shout my name but couldn't turn my head to look at him as the world began to go dark. "Let her go!"

Davina's face floated into the narrowing circle of my vision. "Which way is the light coming from?"

With the last of my strength, I pointed toward Jober's right.

"It's time to cross over, you damn fool," she gave him a hard shove.

Jober stumbled sideways, dragging me along with him.

Uh oh. My feet skidded a few inches across the floor before Drew's arms came around me.

Someone shouted, "Hold her!"

"I am," Drew answered, then whispered in my ear. "I've got you."

Except he didn't because as Davina tried to force Jober into the light, it felt like my soul might rip in half. White light broke over my face and dazzled my vision. This was it. I was about to be killed by a ghost. Just my luck.

But then, her face a mask of concentration and fury, Davina mustered up every ounce of energy she had. She latched onto me with both hands, drove her foot into Jober's hip for one final push. His hand slid off my throat as his body flattened like he'd been steamrollered, and the light sucked him in. Or that's how it looked to me moments before I passed out.

Despite his attempt to recant, Walker's confession held up—mostly because the cops found the rolling pin with his DNA on it. His abrupt exit from the bank spelled good things for Mr. Herbert, who was asked to return to work and given the promotion he deserved.

One week after the arrest, and the unexpected airing of my truth, I skipped our Friday night dinner because Neena was still making excuses not to be around me. She'd asked David to take her home almost immediately after Jober went into the light, and I hadn't seen either of them since. David had messaged me a couple of times just to check in, but he hadn't asked me to help out at the inn, so I took that as a sign to keep my distance from him, too.

I hadn't gone near the shop all week because that was Neena's place, and I didn't want to make her uncomfortable there. Maybe she'd be fine once she'd had time to process, or maybe she wouldn't.

It took three days to get my voice back and longer to stop reliving the experience in my dreams. So much for Drew's plan to keep me from getting hurt again, but the loss of Neena's friendship was more painful than the injury to my throat.

There hadn't been a single sign of Davina since she'd saved my life. Whether that meant she'd gone into the light with Jober or had expended so much energy she needed more time to recharge was anybody's guess.

I knew I should get back into the swing of things and start hunting her killer again, but I couldn't muster enough concern to get started. Instead, I shut everyone out except for my new best friends—Ben and Jerry.

When Patrea showed up on Sunday, I'd been wearing the same ratty yoga pants and sweatshirt for a couple of days. My hair hung in lank strings, and Drew had given up trying to talk me into showering or putting on something nicer. With his hair ruffled from repeatedly running his hands through it and several days' growth of whiskers, he looked as frazzled as I felt.

"You've got company. Maybe Patrea can do something to get you out of this funk," he said once he'd led her to where I'd holed up on the new sofa.

"You look like something the dog dragged out from under a rotten log," Patrea greeted me with the truth.

"Thanks." I didn't offer her a drink or ask her to sit down.

She leaned in for a closer look. "Is that a Skittle stuck to your shirt?"

I shrugged. "Maybe." Looking down, I saw the red blob clinging to the fabric. It made a scratchy noise when I picked it off. Patrea made a gagging sound when I popped it in my mouth.

"That's disgusting. Don't you think you've wallowed long enough?"

The short answer was no. Patrea didn't accept the short answer. Instead, she yanked the fuzzy, purple throw off my lap and half dragged me off the sofa. "You took care of me when I needed it. Now, it's my turn to do the same, so you'll be taking a shower and putting on something that doesn't smell so bad it makes my eyes water, and then we're going to the Blue Moon, where you will buy me pie, and we will eat it while you weep with gratitude for my heroic effort in coming to save your sorry butt."

Patrea meant business. Anyone with eyes could see that, so I did as she said because I didn't want to find out what would happen if I didn't. I wouldn't put it past her to spray me down with air freshener and drag me out of the house.

"Are you happy now?" I asked when I returned, wearing faded jeans and another sweatshirt that was at least all in one piece. While I'd been gone, she'd taken it upon herself to clean up my nest of empty candy wrappers.

In response, she narrowed her eyes and went to the closet for my longest coat. "Put this on. It will cover up that affront to fashion."

I glared at her but ended up in a booth at the diner anyway.

"Neena will come around," Patrea said once she'd ordered for both of us. "Why didn't you tell me?"

I'd been dreading that question ever since Davina blew my cover. Mainly because I didn't have a good answer. "I don't know. I guess I didn't want you to look at me like Neena did. The way everyone else will when the news gets around. If it hasn't already."

"All right. Do you see anyone looking at you like that now?"

"No."

And that was it. She let the subject go.

"I'm closing on the flip house tomorrow."

Because it was there, I took a bite of the custard pie Patrea had ordered for me. "That was quick."

She smiled. "That's what happens when you pay cash and bypass the real estate rigamarole. Who does Leo use for roofing? And I'll need a reputable finish carpenter, too."

I gave Patrea the names and let her distract me with descriptions of the work she planned. When she dropped me off at home, she followed me to the front door and let her guard down for a rare moment.

"You know I love you, right? So don't disappear on me again, okay? I don't do well when someone I care about drops off the map. Next time you throw a pity party, I expect an invitation."

How could one statement make me feel both better and worse?

"I'm sorry. It won't happen again."

Patrea hugged me, then shoved me toward the door. "Go inside and put that man out of his misery. He's worried himself sick over you. And call Jacy while you're at it. She lost the coin toss for being the one to come over here and shake you out of your funk, but that doesn't mean she hasn't been worried, too."

Too bad Ben and Jerry didn't make crow-flavored ice cream because I'd probably need to eat at least a pint or two to make things right.

I turned to watch Patrea leave, then slammed my back against the door when Davina popped up a bit too close for comfort.

"If you're finished feeling sorry for yourself, I need your help."

I sighed. A ghost needing my help...story of my life.

~

Thanks for reading!

If you want to know what's next for Everly, keep reading for a preview of Ghost Writer, when a famous face brings more than baggage to Mooselick River—and Everly finds herself with not one but two spirits who refuse to move on.

~Also Available in Audiobook & Paperback Versions~

Quick Author's Note

Writing Haunting Season gave us the perfect excuse to dig a little deeper into Everly's world—and her friendships.

While the ghosts may be fictional, the bonds between characters are rooted in something very real: loyalty, trust, and the occasional argument over baked goods. As a writing duo, we often find ourselves laughing out loud or tearing up during scenes, and this book gave us plenty of both.

We loved showing what happens when Everly is forced to make hard choices for people she cares about—and when she realizes that ghosts aren't the only ones keeping secrets.

Anyway, if you've come this far with us and not decided we're complete and total whackadoodles...and especially if you have, we're offering a chance to sign up for our newsletters— the best place to get new release updates, sales notifications, and other fun content.

You can sign up for ReGina's newsletter and/or Erin's newsletter and as a thank-you gift for hanging out with us, you'll also get a FREE novella that isn't available anywhere else. And of course, we promise not to SPAM your inbox!

Love, hugs, and happy reading,
ReGina & Erin

P. S. If you enjoyed this book, it would be great if you could leave a review or recommendation on Amazon, GoodReads, or BookBub.

Your reviews help indie authors sell more books!

"Score first, stripper second," Patrea warned in case I was doing it wrong.

"Are we talking about the wallpaper or my love life?" I couldn't help teasing, then laughed when she rolled her eyes at me.

"If you have to ask," she teased back, "you're probably missing the point somewhere."

We didn't talk about why I'd been spending so much time helping her with her house-flipping project. She knew I needed the distraction from my falling out with Neena. Also, there was something oddly satisfying about peeling back the layers of old paper to reveal each successive pattern underneath.

Interesting layers so far on this wall. One with pink and white stripes, the next a bunch of chocolate blobs riding across a background of harvest gold—utterly seventies. Under that, splashy pink cabbage roses strewn across a field of dark blue, and the most difficult so far, also pink and stripey, but sprinkled with yellow flowers that never existed in nature.

"It's coming off okay? And you're not overdoing it with your wrist?" Covered in a fine layer of plaster dust and wearing a pair of faded overalls, her hair bundled under a scarf and her eyes wrapped with a set of protective goggles, Patrea put down the pry bar she'd been using and came to check on me.

This DIY warrior looked nothing like the put-together, slightly stuffy attorney who'd helped me during the first days of my divorce. The current version seemed looser, happier, and far more animated. With a new husband and a big move in her recent past, Patrea had come a long way since the day she'd turned up on my doorstep the Christmas before. She'd settled into small-town living like she'd been born to it. I liked to think I had something to do with the changes.

"So far, but it's a lot of layers." Five, to be exact. I pointed toward the section where I'd made the most progress. "And my wrist is fine. Doesn't even hurt anymore. But should there be cloth underneath the paper? And should it be crunchy?"

Going in for a closer look, Patrea nodded. "That's an old sheet and was probably applied using homemade wheat paste. You can tell by the color as it ages."

"Wheat paste?"

"Flour, sugar, and water, basically. Boiled together, they form a thick glue."

"Huh. You learn something new every day," I said as my phone beeped to signal an incoming text.

"Jacy?" Patrea questioned when I checked to see who it was from, and I shook my head.

It wasn't that my oldest friend, Jacy, had chosen her business partner over me when Neena decided she couldn't handle my ability to see ghosts; that wasn't Jacy's way. I had been the one to pull back because I didn't want to put her in the middle of a problem that had nothing to do with her.

"It's Delilah Cannon."

"Who?" With tender care, Patrea pried off a length of baseboard, crowed with pleasure when it came off intact.

"Davina Benet's former doppelganger."

Flipping the board over, Patrea tapped her hammer against a nail to push it back through the front far enough to grab with the forked end of the prybar. "Davina had a doppelganger? How did I not hear about this before?"

I remembered why. "She popped up here at Halloween when you were in, you know." I flipped my hand to keep from saying the word jail. Plus, now that Patrea knew about my ghost issues, I could tell her the entire story, which I did.

"You should have seen the look on Martha's face when Davina got all spookified and busted up her little publicity stunt. I know it's not nice to laugh at people's misfortune, and you know I appreciate everything Martha has done for me, but I made an exception because she totally brought that comeuppance on herself."

While Patrea laughed along with me, I could practically see the questions dancing around in her head, but the only one she let out was, "Why's this Delilah person texting you now?" She nodded toward the phone I still held in my left hand.

I glanced at the screen to double-check my facts.

"She says she's writing a book about Davina."

Patrea's brows shot up. "Really?" She drew the word out long.

"A tell-all, she says. And she's asked me to find her a place to stay in Mooselick River so she can be closer to Davina's spirit while she works on it."

"Davina's spirit? Does that mean what I think it means?"

"No," I shook my head. "She doesn't have a clue Davina's still hanging around here."

"Okay, so this should be interesting."

"You have no idea." I sent a text back saying I'd look into it for her and followed up with a request for the timing of her plans. "Delilah was Davina's biggest fan, but the admiration was a one-way thing."

I put my phone away and went back to stripping wallpaper while Patrea finished pulling nails, slashed a number three on the back of the baseboard, and stacked it with the rest. "You're numbering them because you plan to put them back?"

Nodding, Patrea moved on to the next. "Yes, that's right, but back to Delilah. I'm fascinated by this book-writing plan. I wonder what Davina will think of it."

"That's the million-dollar question, and I haven't got a clue what the answer will be. I haven't seen much of Davina since the night we took Martin Walker down. In a way, I find that worrisome."

A short silence followed before Patrea said, "Why?"

I shrugged. "She got way into helping Jober cross over, which did not turn out so well for me. And then, that same day you dragged me out of the house, she popped back up asking for my help with another spirit she ran into, but I couldn't help because of how my ghost thing works."

"Explain, please." Fascinated, Patrea gave me her full attention.

"Not much to tell, really. I consulted a psychic, and according to her, Leandra's meddling opened some kind of psychic door or something and probably set up some ridiculous beacon that lets spirits on this side of the veil find and haunt me."

As usual, Patrea clued in when it came to the nuances. Head tilted, she gave me an up-and-down look. "Why are they on this side of the veil? And what does that make you? A medium or a sensitive? Clairvoyant? Is there a difference?"

Shrugging, I said, "According to Kat—that's the medium's name—a true medium can speak to those who have passed behind or beyond the veil. It's an active talent, while mine is more passive. I'm limited to those who are stuck on this side. Like with unfinished business, or whatever. I don't think there's a name for it. I'm haunted."

Patrea mirrored my shrug. "Okay. I guess I see the difference."

Nodding, I continued, "Anyhow, Davina wants to set up some ghost outreach program, and she wants me to help."

"Would that be so bad?"

Only if she decided to make it a lifelong—or rather a death-long—goal. One that would keep her on this side of the veil. In Mooselick River, and in my life.

"It wouldn't, but I have a selfish reason for wanting her to cross over." It felt good to talk about this stuff with someone like Patrea. Despite her absolute acceptance of the esoteric, she was a logical thinker, and always gave thoughtful advice.

When I hesitated to share, she circled a hand to get me to continue. I sighed.

"What I'm about to tell you cannot leave this room, but my mother also has mediumistic tendencies, so part of my ability is inherent. I might have eventually come into my talent on my own, or I might not have. We'll never know because Momma Wade did her hoodoo on me and forced the issue."

"Hoodoo," Patrea repeated. "Good word."

"Right? I think she hexed me to find bodies, too. Makes me feel like a death magnet, but I have no proof that's the case."

Hammer and boards forgotten for the moment, Patrea dug in. "Tell me more. I'm fascinated."

"You've heard most of it," I shrugged. "Basically, I find the body; I see the ghost."

Except for that one time with the haunted pajamas, but even then, there was a tenuous connection between the girl who'd worn them and me. "So far, it's been just the ghosts of murdered people whose bodies I found, or in one case, didn't find, but was near the body shortly after the death."

"Because the spirit was just hanging around waiting for justice." Patrea proved she'd been listening. "And you don't see just any ghost, so you couldn't channel my dead grandmother and ask her where she hid her peach cobbler recipe."

"Not that I know of, but I'm sure Kat would be happy to handle that for you. I'll give you her number if you like."

"Later." For now, Patrea was more interested in my story than in connecting with her relatives. "Did she tell you anything else?"

"Not really. Once I help the dead find justice, they go into the light, and I never see them again, which is fine with me. Or some of them, anyway. Amber hung around awhile."

Patrea slugged me in the arm.

"Ow," I yelped, putting my other hand over the sore spot. "What was that for?"

"For holding out on me. Amber was in the house when I was there at Christmas, wasn't she?"

I nodded. "She had a lot of energy, that one. Used to give me the news every morning before I got out of bed. Complete with the weather report."

"Why didn't you say anything?"

A complicated question, but the answer I gave was simple. "I didn't want you to look at me like Neena did. Does."

"Fair enough, I guess." But I could tell she was hurt that I'd made an assumption about her.

"I'm sorry. If it helps, I wanted to tell you."

"But you didn't. You told Jacy, though, right?"

Oops, another minefield to navigate.

"Yes, but only under extreme circumstances." Because there was no reason not to, I told her how my attempt to help Spencer Charles cross over had put Jacy's life in danger. "And that's why I've been careful about what I say to anyone. I don't want my friends getting hurt on my account."

Patrea's voice went dry as dust. "How noble of you."

"Don't," I pleaded, close to tears. "You don't know what it's like."

"Don't I? I watched you nearly get choked to death by something that shouldn't have been able to touch you, and I couldn't do anything to stop it."

The memory shivered across my skin. "That's the first

time anything like that has happened, and it wasn't on purpose. Davina believes that Jober's complete denial of his death caused something like the ghost version of a psychotic break. I think she's half right. He was already suffering from mental health issues after the death of his family and couldn't handle what happened, so he went over the edge."

"So that doesn't happen every time?"

Solemnly, I shook my head. "Never has before. Or not by a ghost. Hudson's killer tried to choke me to death, but he was just a human jerk. Hudson saved me by rolling one of Catherine's mannequin head down the stairs. Scored a perfect strike."

"Ghost bowling. There's a mental image I never thought I'd have."

"You and me both. I could die happy if people would leave my neck alone. For a second there, I thought I was a goner."

"You and me both, sister." Satisfied with my response, Patrea went back to pulling nails. "That's all very interesting, but you never said what's in it for you when Davina leaves."

"Well, you know that door Leandra opened? Davina thinks she can close it behind her when she goes."

After a short pause, Patrea asked the big question, "Does that mean you wouldn't see ghosts at all anymore?"

"That's her theory, and she knows about my mother

and whatever got passed down through her to me, so I'm hoping Davina actually does know what she's talking about. Not that it matters if she decides not to cross over."

The prying of baseboards stopped. "They can choose to stay?"

"To a point, I guess. I'm no expert on ghostly shenanigans, but Amber didn't leave just because I'd found her killer. I had to make a deal with her to get her to move on. Saved my sanity when she finally went. Besides being my self-appointed news reporter, she lacked a sense of personal space."

I shuddered every time I even thought about the way ghost touches felt.

Patrea noticed my expression. "What's so bad about that?"

"Imagine if you washed the dirtiest, greasiest dishes ever to be used, then left your dishwater in the sink for a week. Nasty, right? With chunks of floating food and muck." Must have been because Patrea grimaced. "Then imagine you put that greasy, scummy mess in the refrigerator to get nice and cold before you dumped it down your back."

Now, it was Patrea's turn to shudder. "Okay, that would be slimy and disgusting."

"Add in the sensation of spiders crawling across your skin, and that's what it feels like to touch a ghost." Because even talking about it evoked the sensation, I shuddered again. "Amber preferred to ignore the rule about keeping her distance."

"There are rules?" Dropping the last baseboard on the pile, Patrea picked up a putty knife to help peel back the layers of wallpaper. "Who makes them?"

"Me. They're mine, and there are only three. No talking to me in public. Amber had trouble with that one, too. Another is that I don't give messages to loved ones. Most of the time, anyway, and they have to respect my personal space, which also includes staying out of my bedroom and bathroom."

Long sheets of paper fell under Patrea's knife. How did she do that? All I could seem to manage were a bunch of small shreds.

"Do you think the messages part is what Neena's having so much trouble with?" And now, Patrea got around to the most painful question. "You held out on her."

It felt like my stomach rolled over. "I gave her the message. I just didn't tell her it was directly from Hudson, but you're right. I held out on her, and I shouldn't have because it cost too much. Still, I'm not sure it's just about that with her. She reacted badly when Viola didn't understand Davina's talent and tried to get her to channel Hudson."

"Neena will come around," Patrea repeated what Jacy had said.

"I hope so, but I'm not counting on anything."

Wisely, Patrea changed the subject and showed me her trick for getting larger sections of wallpaper off at a time. Every so often, she'd give me a measuring look, and I couldn't tell if it had to do with the ghost thing or if she hoped I'd get inspired to do some remodeling of my own.

In the end, it turned out to be neither.

"Chris thinks we're ready to start a family."

I dropped my putty knife, then schooled the surprise out of my expression when I bent hastily to pick it up. "That's big news. What do you think?"

"You know I never expected to fall in love, and it happened so fast."

"Same with Drew and me, so I get it, but does that mean you don't want kids?"

Slowly, Patrea shook her head. "That's the thing. I think I do. I mean, like, I really think I do."

Excited, I nearly beaned her with the scoring tool when I pulled her in for a hug. "That's fantastic. Will you start trying right away? Maybe you and Jacy will be baby-buddies."

"Maybe. Or maybe you could put Drew out of his misery, marry the man, and we could all be baby-buddies together."

"I'm not sure the world is ready for that." If Patrea meant to tease, she missed the mark because I'd been thinking about my future with Drew a lot lately. "We haven't even had our first big fight yet. I think it might be too soon to consider this a forever thing."

Serious now, Patrea turned her full attention on me. "Don't."

"Don't what?"

"Don't measure Drew against what happened with Paul. You're not that young, inexperienced person anymore, and besides, Paul was a predator who knew exactly how to play you. Not because of who you were, but because he'd taken being a sleezebag to an art form. He and Drew are night and day."

"In my heart, I know that's true. My head just doesn't want to catch up."

"Just because things happened fast both times, it doesn't mean your judgment is skewed."

How did she know exactly what I'd been worrying about?

"I guess not. My mother loves Drew, and she never liked Paul. As much as I hate to say it, I trust her judgment more than mine. But there's this other thing. He remembers the first time we met—in detail—while I barely noticed him. Maybe I should have felt something or remembered him more if we were meant to be like soul mates, or whatever."

Patrea snorted. "Or whatever. You're a piece of work, Everly Dupree. So what if you didn't remember meeting some boy for a day when you were just a girl? You love him now, and now is all that matters. Why haven't you had the big fight?"

I frowned. "I don't know."

"Yes, you do." Patrea wasn't having any of that excuse. "Think about it, and don't tell me it's because you agree on everything. If you say that, I will call you a liar, and I might also barf on your shoes. Nice boots, by the way."

We returned to scraping wallpaper while I considered the question, and finally came out with, "We don't agree on everything, but we don't argue. We debate. We discuss. And if we're both tired, we might snap a little at each other. But you can't argue with Drew because he's...I don't know exactly how to put it."

"A suck-up?" Patrea supplied helpfully. "Pushover. Under your thumb."

"No, and that's not very flattering because it makes him sound boring, and he's not. He's just Drew. He has a way of listening to what's under the words and understanding what's inside me. He has plenty of fire in him, but he doesn't turn it into anger and then dump it on the people he loves. He'd rather beat the hell out of a punching bag than argue over who should have unloaded the dishwasher."

"That's all well and good, but it also sucks."

"How do you figure?"

"Isn't it obvious? The lack of make-up sex. You're really missing out there."

My face flamed. Thank you, red hair and light skin. "If

things got any better in that department, I'm not sure I could handle it."

"Okay, then." Patrea let the conversation die, but she allowed herself a smirk and got me thinking, which was probably the point.

Ghost Writer is available now. Keep reading for a preview of the free novella you'll get for joining our newsletters.

Excerpt from A Snowball's Chance in Spell

*L*ightning flirted in shadows of the dark clouds hovering over my house when I came home from work the afternoon before my twenty-second Christmas Eve. Nothing unusual there. With three elemental faeries living in the house, weird weather happened all the time. Or rather, every time my temperamental godmothers mounted some sort of snit.

The godmothers idled at snit.

Going back to work wasn't an option. I'd cleared the last match of the year—a lovely couple with a shared affection for online gaming—and I was no coward. When it came to diffusing faerie fights, I consider myself an expert, and this one didn't look like it rated more than a two on the volcano scale.

Yes, you heard right. I measure faerie fights on the scale of whether or not a volcano might erupt in my backyard. Living with faeries is never boring. Occasionally dangerous—especially because I have yet to come into the magic that is my birthright, but never boring.

A quick check proved they'd contained the madness to the inside and/or the backyard. The two feet of snow on the front lawn was still there and still white—you try explaining black snow to your neighbors sometime. I didn't see any winged denizens—fae or otherwise—dotting the roof ridge, or hear any ominous sounds. If not for the fact that lightning is rare in Maine during the winter, and rarer still when confined to a single area, I'd have thought it was a quiet day in the household.

In my head, I downgraded the threat to a level one, and went inside.

For the most part, my place looks like an ordinary, New England style home. Built by my great grandparents, it's the oldest house in a neighborhood that grew up around it when the suburbs expanded into what was once a rural area. Because, I think, the faeries wanted to give me a normal upbringing, they left the house in mostly the same condition it was in when they came to take care of me and only added on a wing for their own use.

I stepped into the front hall expecting...well, just about anything. Did I mention the faeries love holidays? Maybe they don't have them in the faelands, or maybe they do and go overboard there, too. I can't say since I've never been, but I could tell at a glance there were more decorations than there had been when I left.

"Terra!" I yelled, but got no answer. Terra, faerie of earth, held sway over all the flora and fauna found on dry land. She would be the one responsible for the pine boughs twining over anything that held still long enough. Fire faerie, Soleil, contributed by setting sparks of faerie light to twinkle inside the delicate ice bubbles crafted by her sister, Evian, mistress of water. The effect was lovely, but not as lovely as the three women could be when their faces weren't twisted, as they were now, with rage.

I came upon them in their favorite fighting grounds:

the kitchen. It looked like I'd caught this one early since there was relatively little damage done so far. Steam rose from a puddle of water at Soleil's feet which I assumed had come from Evian. Vines snaked from between the kitchen tiles to twine around Evian's ankles, and there were a few smoking embers dotting Terra's hair. Nothing more than a minor spat.

Keeping it casual, I asked, "What's going on?" There's no rhyme or reason to what will settle a fight or send one into the red zone.

Terra turned one granite pink eye in my direction. "This doesn't concern you." The fingers of her left hand twitched and the vines slithered from Evian's ankles to her knees.

Retaliating, Evian conjured a gush of water from thin air, and doused the smoking embers. The scent of pine boughs couldn't compete with the stench of burnt hair, or the pungent funk erupting from the flowers that burst into bloom near her feet.

"Now look," I pointed out to Terra before she conjured something worse. "Evian is trying to help."

"Was not." Evian snapped her fingers and turned Terra's wet hair white with frost, except because the vines were now questing higher, she overshot the mark and doused a few of Soleil's decorative sparkles.

That was the moment I lost control.

Oh, who am I kidding? I never had control.

Soleil let out a screech and lobbed a fireball at Evian,

who encased it in a ball of water and batted it toward Terra. I felt scoured clean when Terra called all the dirt and dust in the house to form a layer over the bobbing ball of doom which now resembled a small planet whizzing back toward Soleil.

It might have ended better if I'd have kept my mouth shut, but I didn't.

"You're going to put an eye out with that thing."

The ire of three faeries is a potent thing, but not as potent as a flaming mudball. I ducked, rolled, and hit the latch on the patio door in what I'd like to think was a graceful move. Probably looked like a seal rolling off a rock.

The flaming fireball arced over my head, its warm breeze tossing my hair, and rocketed off into the sky.

Crisis averted. Except, it wasn't. I should have known.

A Snowball's Chance in Spell is only available by signing up for one of our newsletters here:
https://reginawelling.com
https://erinlynnwrites.com

If you'd like to meet more people who live rent-free in our heads, here's a list of other series we've written. Our books are all set in fictional towns in Maine, and some characters like to flit back and forth between series. The cast of Psychic Seasons hangs out with Everly and also with Lexi Balefire from the Fate Weaver series. Mag and Clara Balefire are Lexi's grandmother and aunt!

Psychic Seasons
Four women, four love stories, and a whole lot of supernatural surprises. In the quaint town of Oakville, Maine, psychic visions, ghostly whispers, and fate itself conspire to change lives—and hearts—forever

Haunted Everly After
Everly Dupree came home for a fresh start—not a full-time gig solving ghostly murders. But when the dearly departed start demanding justice, what's a reluctant medium to do?

Ponderosa Pines Mysteries
Nothing bad ever happens in the weird little town of Ponderosa Pines...until someone dies. Now it's up to best friends Chloe and EV to solve the mystery—before the town's secrets bury them too.

Fate Weaver
Lexi Balefire—matchmaker, witch, and accidental fate-weaver—must balance love, magic, and a family legacy of chaos before destiny decides for her!

Mag and Clara Balefire Mysteries
Sister witches Mag and Clara Balefire move to a sleepy Maine town for a fresh start—only to find themselves conjuring up trouble, solving murders, and keeping their magic under wraps in this charmingly witchy cozy mystery series

Laurel Haven Witches
Four witches, destined by blood and magic, must embrace their power, battle a dark legacy, and surrender to the love that could break the curse—or bind them to it forever.

Nell Page: Accidental Investigator
Nell Page owns a bookstore, drinks too much coffee, and has a habit of noticing things she probably shouldn't. With warmth, wit, and an accidental talent for

investigating, Nell tackles mysteries that don't always involve murder—but always matter.

www.ingramcontent.com/pod-product-compliance
Lightning Source LLC
Chambersburg PA
CBHW061526210726
48287CB00006B/1851